## AN EROTIC PARODY

**DICK BUSH**

**BYTE I**
# INFINITY WELCOMES SEXY DRIVERS

# 1

Residents of all the moons of Saturn had a reputation for being rather stuck up and posh. Mimas was prime real estate and only the very wealthiest of families could afford to live there. The terraforming of nearly every solid planet and moon in the solar system had taken a good couple of hundred years to complete and the maintenance of the giant factories, which kept the air breathable and the land fertile was run by your basic workmen. Blue collar, hard working guys and girls, working hard to keep everyone on their particular planet alive. And boy did they love to unwind at the end of the day.

Strip clubs were looked down upon by the rich upper class of Mimas and were incredibly scarce on the surface of the moon. However a few hundred miles above the surface was a different story all together.

The travelling strip club spaceship, Pink Dwarf, pulled into dock at the Titan 3 space-station. It was grey in appearance with the huge company logo, which also served as the name of the ship, slapped on the side.

Deb Lister knew she was going to have a very profitable night and made sure she picked out the very sluttiest of stripper boots she owned. Her bunk was a mess and it got messier the more clothes she threw out onto the floor. She was looking for a particular top. The strappy one with nipple holes but couldn't find it anywhere.

'Fuck it,' she said and walked out of her room wearing

only her thigh high black boots and a tiny black thong.

Lister walked past the other bunk rooms where the girls lived and headed to the main dance area towards the back of the ship. Music was blasting out louder than usual. The ship's computer, Hab had assumed the duties of DJ and compare since the last guy went space crazy after a twelve week jaunt to Pluto. His bald disembodied head bounced around the large screen above the stage and saw Deb walking in.

'Ok everyone,' Hab said. 'Please welcome Deb Lister onto the stage!'

Deb climbed onto the stage. The place was already packed and she could see bodies everywhere. Every girl on the ship must have been working. It was the busiest it's ever been.

As a dirty sexy music track started, Deb worked the pole like a sex monger. Rubbing her arse against the metal shaft and making sure to look at all the gawpers around the stage in the eye. One of them was going to tip her big. Somewhere in that sea of people was someone with a card full of dollar-pounds that had her name on it.

Her dance moves drove the crowd wild. Her long black silky hair flicked about and the highlights she had done only a few days ago glowed neon pink and then green and then blue.

Lister got to her knees and crawled across the stage as she spied one guy. He wasn't yelling, like the others. He was just looking. Watching. Mesmerised. She crawls right up to him and grabs hold of his collar and licks her tongue over his lips and nose. He lets out a sigh of amazement.

'Oh baby,' he said. 'I gotta get a dance with you.'

Lister moved her lips to his ear and spoke in her rich Liverpudlian accent. 'If you've got the dollar-pounds, I'll give you much more than a dance.'

He gulped. 'Hell yeah.'

The music finished and everyone applauded. None more so than the gawper covered in Lister's saliva. Lister held out her hand for him to take and she hopped off the stage and walked him to the back of the room.

'Give it up for Deb Lister,' Hab said, sliding on a pair of

black shades. 'One of our most eager of dancers. Oh she'd get it. This is what I'd do... I'd rub my nose right on her clit.' Hab started rolling his head back and forth, staring into an imaginary vagina in front of his face. 'Like that... oh yeah... then... a little bit of tongue.' Hab flicked his tongue out and closed his eyes. 'Oh fuck yeah... that's the stuff.'

Captain Tau stood at the back of the room and watched the screen as her ship's computer continued demonstrating the art of the nose-job to anyone willing to watch. She was a tall woman with a commanding presence and booming voice, especially when angry.

'Rimmer,' she shouted.

Reginald Rimmer, a tall slim man, ran over to the Captain. He wore an ill fitting grey suit, baggy shirt and shoes that looked far too big for him.

'Yes, mon Capitaine?' Rimmer said.

'What have I told you about that damn computer? Get him to introduce the girls. That's it. No more of that.' She pointed at the screen and Rimmer turned to see Hab pretending to push his head in between a pair of large imaginary breasts.

'I'd love to push my head right in between them,' Hab said. 'Like that.'

Rimmer beamed a smile of innocence. 'Of course,' he said. 'He probably just needs a reboot. I'll get on it right away.' Another huge smile exploded from Rimmer's face and hit Tau directly between the eyes. She sighed and walked away from him. She couldn't stand incompetence and Rimmer oozed it. His job was a simple one. Run the strip club. Make sure girls were on the stage when they needed to be. Make sure the bar is stocked. Everything else pretty much ran itself. A monkey could do it. In fact Pink Dwarf's biggest rival ship, The Tenshi had a particularly hard working Mandrill running their club. Perhaps she should make him an offer.

Lister pushed her firm butt cheeks onto the guy's crotch. The private dance area consisted of twenty little nooks which were curtained off. It felt classier than the electronic hissing doors outside of the club area and made the punters feel relaxed. Like they could be sat in a club on terra firma. Not that Lister cared. All she wanted was the money. And none of the girls made as much dollar-pounds as she did. She had put the money to good use and spent it on bodily upgrades. Her breasts had the size adjustment option built in and also acted as airbags if involved in a vehicle accident or particularly nasty fall. She'd never forgotten the time when they saved her life on Ganymede when she had gotten so incredibly drunk, she passed out in a swimming pool and awoke the next morning bobbing about, tits keeping her afloat.

She turned around to face the client and shoved her tits in his face.

'Bigger? Smaller? Softer?' she asked.

'Really big.... and really soft,' he said.

Lister pushed her finger against the side of the boobs and made a circle motion with it. Her breasts started inflating to their maximum size. Twice what they were. They became soft and pendulous and the client started nuzzling them.

She reached down to his crotch and felt his hard little soldier in his pants. She unzipped him and set it free. Lister pulled back and stood before him. She turned around and very slowly, with her feet together, pulled down her tiny black thong all the way to her ankles. Her pussy gleamed with a silky shine and she ran a finger back up her leg and pushed her hand between her thighs. She ran her finger over the lips of her pussy and pushed a finger inside, dipping it in and pulled it out, taking a good load of pussy juice with it. She turned back around and licked her finger, watching the guy stare at her with lust. His cock was rock solid now.

Lister got on all fours and crawled up to him. Her face was inches away from his penis. She knew he could feel her breath on it.

'Come on, let's see the money,' she said.

He reached into his pocket and pulled out a prepay card with a limit of 500 dollar-pounds. 'Well how much did you say?'

Lister eyed the card and snatched it out of his hand. 'Yep, that'll do.'

'But that's...' Lister pushed her mouth over his cock and deep throated him. 'Oh fuck, that's worth it.' Lister continued to ram her head down on his crotch. She could feel his bell-end pushing against her throat. She pulled her head up and spat down on her large, squishy boobs. She wrapped them around his cock and started gently moving them up and down. 'Oh my fucking god, you're amazing.'

'Yeah, I'm pretty fucking awesome,' Lister said.

His spunky load blew across her breasts and he sat there, quivering as if he'd never come so hard before. Lister licked the spunk from the tip of his cock and gave him a quick extra suck.

The curtains behind her suddenly flew open and she turned to see Rimmer stood there, mouth wide open in utter shock.

'Um, Lister,' he said. 'Is that a client's penis, you're sucking off in the private dance room?'

'No, it's a chicken,' Lister said.

'Come with me, right now.'

'Smeg.' Lister dialled back her boobs to normal size and wiped the spunk from her chest.


The front of the ship housed the managerial staff, cockpit and Captain's quarters. The mid-section was where the staff set navigational courses and booked in certain planets and moons to dock at. Lister rarely saw this area and it strange to see it as a working spaceship; she really only saw it as her home and workplace.

Captain Tau stood in front of Lister; her tall stature dwarfed her. Lister had put on her tight leather trousers and had managed to find a black top which just about managed to cover most of her breasts.

'Dammit Lister, I've told you about this,' she said.

'Captain, I didn't want to do it,' Lister said, putting on her most innocent of looks. 'He offered me money, lots of money.'

Saunders, the second in command, turned to Lister. His

red uniform was a shimmering flurry of light. The bright H on his forehead showed that he was a hologram; a dead member of the crew brought back in holographic form using his saved memory.

'Then why are these all over the outernet?' Saunders said, pointing at the view screen behind him. The screen showed an advert showing Lister sucking a giant cock with her thumbs up. The caption beside it read *I love sucking cock*.

'It was just the one time,' Lister said.

Saunders nods to the screen and it fades to another advert showing Lister wanking off two guys either side of her with the caption, *I'll suck your cock for money. I do it all the time*.

'I just needed some extra cash,' Lister said.

'No wonder we've been getting so many customers,' Saunders said.

'You're going to stasis, Lister,' Tau said. 'For the rest of the tour.'

'No, please, I need the money. You can't,' Lister said. Stasis meant missing the next four weeks they were going to be stationed at Mimas and the next two weeks they had planned at Titan. It was a disaster. Her breasts were on finance and if she didn't pay them off every month, robot repo men were sure to turn up at her airlock and rip them out of her body while she was still conscious.

'It's in your contract, Lister,' Saunders said. 'You broke the rules.'

'"You're just pissed off because you're a hologram,' Lister said. 'The only thing you can touch is yourself.'

'That's it,' Tau said. 'Rimmer, take her to stasis.' Rimmer stepped forward and rook Listers arm as if he were an arresting police officer.

'It would be my pleasure,' he said and raised his hand in an elegantly over the top salute that lasted a good five seconds.

'And Saunders,' Tau said. 'Have we found that cat yet?'

'Not yet Captain, Hab thinks he may have gone down to the storage area.'

Rimmer walked Lister into the stasis room and up to one of the vertical person sized pods inside.

'So what exactly does this thing do?' Lister asked.

'Know anything about quantum mechanics?'

'Well I did once watch a porno with midgets,' Lister said as the pod door opened and Rimmer motioned for her to enter.

'As soon as the stasis field comes down, time will no longer be passing for you. You'll be a frozen instant in time. But for you, no time will have passed. And I wont have to deal with your insubordination any longer.' He smiled and tapped a few buttons on the control panel outside the pod. Lister stepped in and turned to Rimmer.

'Rimmer,' she said. 'Admit it, you're just jealous it wasn't your cock I was taking down my throat.'

Rimmer mashes his palm into the key pad and the pod door hissed shut. 'Activate the stasis field Hab.'

'Stasis field activated,' Hab said.

A bright energy field shone down over Lister as she raised her fist to give Rimmer the middle finger. Her movement slowed to a complete stop and she hung there completely motionless giving a big fuck you to anyone who would walk inside the room.

# 2

Lister watched as the bright beam of light sone down on her inside the stasis tube. She raised her arm and stuck her middle finger up at Rimmer who suddenly sped out of the room at a ridiculously fast rate. The beam of light stopped and the door to the pod swung open. Typical, she thought. Nothing on this ship worked properly.

'Rimmer?' she said, stepping out of the pod. There was silence. Just the constant hum of the ship's engines. No music. No chatter. For a ship containing fifty strippers that was just plain impossible.

'It's safe to come out now Deb,' Hab's voice said.

Lister walked into the corridor and made her way towards the front of the ship. It was eerie how still and quiet things were. She assumed it must be the middle of the night, ship time. But even then half the crew would be awake.

'Where is everyone Hab?' she asked.

'They're dead, Deb.'

'What do you mean, they're dead?'

'A few hours after you went into stasis, my system was rebooted. When I came back online there had been a critical meltdown in one of the core engines, causing a radiation leak.'

'Smeg,' Lister said as she stepped into the mid-section and looked around at all the empty chairs and blank computer screens. Hab dissolved into view on the large screen in front of her.

'Is everyone ok?' she asked.

'The blast wave annihilated every living thing in it's path, Deb. The only thing I could do to prevent the risk of it spreading to the space station and surrounding ships was to detach Pink Dwarf and set us off full speed into deep space.'

'Well how far away from Mimas are we now, Hab?'

'Well... I had to wait a while for the radiation to subside before letting you out.'

'How long?'

'Three million years,' Hab said, calmly.

'Three million years?' Lister said. 'I missed Game of Thrones.' She couldn't believe it. It was on it's 209th season and the finale was due to be broadcast a couple of days after she went into stasis. She sighed and sat on the navigation officer's chair. 'So that's it? Just me? All alone?"

'Well,' Hab said. 'Kinda.'

'What do you mean... Kinda?'

Rimmer walked in wearing a familiar shimmering red uniform made entirely of photons. He had a glowing red H on his forehead.

'Hello Lister,' he said.

'Oh what the smeg,' Lister said, looking Rimmer up and down. 'Out of all the people you could have brought back as a hologram, you bring back Rimmer?' Lister swung her foot into his groin and passed straight through his holographic body.

'His was the only personality disk that wasn't damaged,' Hab said.

'What personality?' Lister said. 'Oh this is bad.' She got up and paced around the room.

'Bad?' said Rimmer. 'I'm the one who can't touch anything except myself.'

'At least your sex life wont change. I can't handle this... just me and him for the rest of my life?'

'Well... kinda,' Hab said.


Lister and Rimmer exited the turbo lift and stepped out into the cargo deck. The shelves stood several stories high and were supposed to contain all manor of food and supplies.

Except the shelves were completely empty. All around them were makeshift houses; a tiny shanty town strewn across the entire deck. There were gardens with trees, vegetables even a large pond. The entire deck had been transformed into a living ecosystem.

Lister raised her wrist and spoke into her watch, which showed Hab floating about on the screen.

'So this cat changed into human form in three million years?' Lister said.

'I managed to seal most of the radiation away from the cargo deck... but it seems the cats mutated.'

'Cats?" said Rimmer. 'Plural?'

'Just one left now,' Hab said. 'She mostly hides down here.'

'She?' said Rimmer, suddenly excited.

'She's a cat, Rimmer,' Lister said. 'She's not going to be...' Lister stopped mid sentence as the Cat stepped out from the shadows in front of them. '...hot.'

She was a gorgeous petite woman with incredible curves, slim waist and a devastating chest. Her long blonde hair was immaculate and so seductively worn. It cascaded down over the side of face, perfectly framing her dark eye makeup and full pouty lips. She wore long black shiny boots, slim black leggings and a tiny crop top that barely kept her enormous, gravity defying breasts inside.

Lister was stunned at how brave she was. She walked right up to her, eyeing her up and down and rubbed her head against her chest.

'Oh you're nice,' Cat said. 'Yeah, I like you. If you feed me, I'll let you stroke me? Huh? How about it?' She licked Lister's face and continued to push her head against her breasts and paw at her skin.

'Ok, sure,' Lister said and gave her a stroke on her head, which the cat seemed to really enjoy.

'Ok, this is getting weird,' Rimmer said, scowling at the two women who continued to caress and fawn over each other.

'Well it has been three million years since I got laid,' Lister said.

Rimmer placed his hands on his knees and bent over, as though talking to a child. 'Hey kitty, how about you come upstairs with us, hey?'

Cat turned to Rimmer and hissed.

'Fine, do what you want,' Rimmer said and walked back to the turbo lift.

Cat started kissing and licking the side of Lister's neck. She had been with plenty of women. She had even put on girl on girl shows for guys in the club but this woman was so totally different from anyone she'd ever met before. She obviously hadn't had much company in a while. Every touch of her skin, every caress of her body seemed to make her purr. Lister smiled and cradled her head in her hands, running her fingers through her luscious hair. Cat smiled back and ran her hands over Lister's breasts, making her nipples hard. The sensation seemed to run all the way down her spine to her pussy and she could feel herself getting wet with excitement.

'You smell good,' Cat said.

'You do too.' Lister pushed her hand onto Cat's breasts. They felt so soft but looked as though they were surgically implanted to be perfect. No scarring though. They were 100% real and impossibly perfect.

Cat pulled up her top and showed her erect nipples to Lister and smiled again. Lister wrapped her arms around her and pushed her lips onto her breasts. She flicked her tongue over the pink perfect buds of flesh and sucked. Cat moaned out loud and Lister reached down to her buttocks and grabbed them. They were fleshy and pert, just like her boobs, yet firm and incredibly biteable.

Lister pushed her hands inside her leggings and touched her bare flesh. She ran her hand further down, until it pushed between her legs. Cat's pussy was soaking wet and Lister gently ran a finger over her clit, causing Cat to moan even more and her legs to nearly give way.

Lister sped up her movement and Cat bent over slightly and pulled up Lister's top, releasing her breasts. Cat started sucking on them as Lister pushed a finger inside her pussy and fucked her hard. Cat's buttocks wobbled with every movement that Lister made with her arm and she felt Cat's warm tongue on her nipples making her pussy get wetter and wetter.

Lister pulled her finger out of Cat, who grabbed it and started licking the juices off it. Cat slowly got to her knees and took hold of Lister's leather trousers in her teeth. She pulled the fly open and slowly peeled the leather material down her legs, revealing the tiny thin thong she was wearing. Cat bit it and held it in her teeth and slowly pulled it away from Lister's pussy. She released it from her mouth and moved in close and took a deep breath through her nose, smelling her scent. She pulled the thong to one side and ran her tongue the full length of her warm pink flesh. She did it one more time, deeper than before and continued lapping at her pussy, over and over. Lister could feel the orgasm coming; she steadied herself by reaching out to one of the shelving structures next to her and breathed heavily as the sensation rolled over her body. Wave after wave of orgasmic pleasure radiated from her groin. She felt the sweat dripping from her back and chest and had to lean against the shelving structure to prevent herself from falling over. This creature may have been alone for a long time, but she definitely knew what she was doing.

'Where did you learn how to do that?' Lister asked.

'Movies,' Cat said, licking her lips. Lister joined her on the floor.

'So you basically hang out down here and watch porn all day?' Lister said. 'That explains a lot.'

Cat turned onto all fours and stuck her arse in the air. 'I want you inside me,' she said.

'Ok, little kitty cat, I'll teach you something those movies never will,' Lister said. 'How to come harder than you ever have before.'

Cat smiled and nodded in delight. Lister pulled down Cat's leggings so there were around her knees and knelt behind her. She pushed her face into her warm pussy and slowly ran her tongue over her clit. Cat responded by moaning gently and pushing back into Lister's face. She increased her speed and pushed two fingers inside her moist

13

pussy as she kept on licking at her clit. She brought her head away and pushed another finger inside her. She found the right spot. The spot that made the audible moaning stop and Cat was just mouthing orgasmic screams. It was so intense she couldn't vocalise anything. Lister smiled and carried on, faster and harder. Cat's pussy was now dripping with juices as she pounded her little fists on the ground and let out an almighty howl of ecstasy. Lister pulled her fingers out of her and flurry of warm liquid sprayed out of her pussy, covering Lister's chest and face.

Cat fell to the ground and turned onto her back. 'I can feel it,' she said. 'It's coming out.'

'What's coming out?'

'I want it inside you,' she said and opened her legs wide, exposing her gaping little pussy. It started to twitch and pulsate. Lister squinted her eyes, trying to make out what the hell was happening to her. With a splutter of pussy juice something pushed it's way out of her tight little hole. It was fleshy and semi turgid as it poked its head out and continued to grow. Lister couldn't believe what she was seeing. Cat was growing a penis out of her pussy. The thick pink cock was covered in her juices and stood a good eight inches high. Lister was well aware of expensive procedures to get something like that done. In fact many of the top escorts of the moons of Jupiter had the ability to be either male or female; double the client base, it made sense. But Lister had never heard of it being natural. Is this what three million years worth of radiation does to a species?

Cat's freshly grown enormous penis quivered and Lister's pussy started drool at the sight of it. She didn't care how different it was, she had always been happy to explore and try new things. She reached out and took hold of it. Cat moaned and arched her back slightly. It felt warm and muscular as she stroked it up and down. She imagined it inside her and knew it would hit the right place. She leaned forward and licked from her pussy, all the way up the shaft of her cock and saw Cat's eyes close as she enjoyed the sensation.

Lister positioned herself next to Cat and swung her right

leg over her body, so her pussy was directly above her face. She felt a tongue play with her pussy and looked down at the girthy meat stick in front of her. Lister leaned forward towards it and the juices from inside cat's pussy filled Lister's mouth as she moved her lips over the end of it and slowly took it deep into her mouth. Cat arched her back again, pushing it deeper to the back of Lister's throat.

Lister held Cat's legs and pulled herself deep onto her cock. She could feel it pulsate inside her, growing with every push. She slowly pulled her head away and watched it gently slide out of her throat and mouth. It had grown to a good eleven inches now and Lister's eyes widened. She had to have this thing inside her.

Lister dismounted Cat's face and swung herself around, climbing back on top of her, this time face to face. She hovered above the huge pulsating tip of Cat's cock and slowly lowered herself onto it. She felt it fill her up inside as the wetness from her lips dripped down the sides of Cat's cock. She rocked back and forth, slowly building momentum and pushed herself down hard onto her petite frame. Cat let out a cry of satisfaction and Lister fucked her harder, writhing her hips forward and back, faster and harder. Sweat dripped from her face onto Cat's chest as the orgasm started inside her. Everything went blank. All she could think of was the pleasure. She kept going, harder, faster, faster and harder until the sensation was too much. Lister let out a cry of orgasmic pleasure and collapsed down ontop of Cat, who held her tightly and slowly dipped her cock in and out of her pussy, gently.

Lister moaned again as Cat started to fuck her harder once more. She felt so incredibly sensitive but it felt too good to stop. Cat pushed the entire length of her cock into Lister over and over and with another cry of euphoric wailing and shuddered suddenly. Lister pulled her body off cat's pulsing shaft and Cat squeezed her eyes shut. Spunk erupted from her cock and shot across Lister's bare back with explosive aplomb. Cat howled as more and more spunk shot out of her, covering Lister's buttocks. She felt it drip down the sides of her legs and slowly got off Cat and laid down next to her utterly exhausted and utterly satisfied.

Cat wiped the sweat from her brow and sat up, looking at Lister. 'So, can you feed me now?'

Rimmer paced around the mid-section as Hab looked on.

'You're saying we haven't traveled in exactly a straight line, then?' Rimmer said.

Hab shook his head. 'No such thing as straight lines when it comes to interstellar space travel. It's all gravitational lensing and special relativity out here.'

'Right... in English please Hab.'

'I don't know where we are.'

'No clue?'

'Well I know we're approximately three million years from our solar system and I'm fairly certain it's still behind us.'

'Three million years away?'

'But if I'm off by even a single degree, we'd still miss it by light years.'

'You're not the greatest ship computer, are you Hab?'

'Well I did always consider myself DJ and compare first and intergalactic navi-computer second.'

'Aren't you supposed to keep records of where we've been? You know... maps and all that?'

'Well I made a chart of all the moons we passed that resembled arses. If that helps?'

'I have to be honest with you Hab, it doesn't help a bit... But I'll take a look at those charts anyway.'

'I remember passing a moon that looked like a Kardashian's arse about three thousand years ago. I suppose I could just work my way back. Hop from arse-moon to arse-moon. As soon as we get to Jennifer Lawrence 13, I think I can probably work out the rest of the way.'

Lister and Cat walked into the mid-section, fully dressed but glowing and still rather sweaty. Rimmer turned from one of the video screens and looked at the state of them.

'Oh look, little miss horny returns with her play thing. Disgusting. It's a good thing you never had a pet, Lister. The RSPCA would be all over you.'

'She's human,' Lister said. 'Look at her. Tell him Hab.'

Cat hopped up onto one of the desks and took out a pocket mirror. She started running her hands through her hair and fixing her makeup.

'She's right Reginald,' Hab said. 'Just as you were a human evolved from primates, she is a human evolved from cats.'

Rimmer made a disgruntled grunting sound and crossed his arms unable to come up with any kind of witty comeback.

'See? Human,' Lister said. 'And if she's human, then there may be others.'

Cat suddenly perked up and looked over at Lister. 'Men?'

'Men,'Lister said.

'Oh for god's sake,' Rimmer said.

'Hab, plot a course for Earth,' Lister said, putting her arm around Cat. 'We're going home.'

## BYTE II
# TYTEN

# 1

Reginald Rimmer watched as Deb Lister's attempt to give him the finger froze in time. She was going to be stuck like that for weeks and Rimmer couldn't be more happy about it. She made his life a misery. It was his job to manage the strip club area of the ship but Lister one one of those kind of people that you meet and instantly want to buy them a toaster. For their bath.

She had, on countless occasions, mocked him, challenged his authority and coerced other girls into doing the same. He had become a joke, all thanks to her. Even the Captain and the crew looked down on him. He knew he was seen as incompetent and socially awkward. It hadn't always been like that. In his youth Rimmer would always be out with his friends. Sure, they'd also make jokes about his hair or clothes or his virginity but it was boisterous fun and he was still included in the jokes. On the ship, people smiled to his face and then made jokes about his behind his back. There was a huge difference.

Now that Lister was safely tucked away in stasis it was time to make a change. He was going to earn some respect on Pink Dwarf. By the end of the week it was his goal to have everyone on board making jokes at his expense in front of his face. Where they should be.

He walked through the long corridor, which connected the front, navigation and drive room areas of the ship to the middle sleeping quarters section and the strip club area at the back of the ship.

The club was still thumping with music and the rest of the girls were working hard, gyrating on top of punters or swinging around the shiny metal poles. He lived and worked on a ship where sexuality was the main focus. The crew and girls all mingled in the evenings. Every one of them had been laid by one of the dancers at some point or another. Everyone except him. He had watched Navigation Officer Donaldson flirt with Rachel; she was so incredibly out of his league. The way he expertly talked to her, drew her in, was in itself memorising. Rimmer had been reading a book on how to pick up women uses mentalism and today he was determined to test it out.

Hab was bopping along to the music on his video screen above the DJ booth. His background was awash with naked women, all jumping up and down in slow motion. Rimmer walked through the club and looked around. Stephanie was leaning by the bar, not talking to anyone. Rimmer had always fancied her. He'd always fancied all of them. Probably because he knew he could never have them. But things were going to change. He wanted to be seen as different. Powerful. More in control. He casually strolled over to Stephanie and leaned next to her.

He almost immediately realised he had misjudged the angle of his lean. His elbow was resting on the bar top but his feet were at least a meter away from the rest of him. Stephanie looked over at him and looked down at his feet and then up at his face.

'What are you doing?' she said.

'Ahh, just taking it all in, you know?'

'Right.'

'Great ship, isn't it. I mean really great.'

'It's a piece of shit. Everything breaks. Doors don't open. The engines fail constantly. And that damn bloody computer keeps getting my name wrong.'

'Ah yes, Hab... I'm on that actually. Heading down to the server room to give him a bit of reboot.'

'So he'll get my name right from now on?' She turned to Rimmer, looking hopeful. Rimmer had never seen a woman look at him with hope in her eyes. It was usually the other way around.

'Absolutely. In fact... to make it up... you can keep 100% of your earnings for tomorrow night. The house takes nothing.' Rimmer smiled and slowly walked his feet back towards the bar so his head finally came eye to eye with Stephanie.

'Are you serious? That would be amazing?' She reached out and touched his shoulder. She actually touched him. He was on a roll... he couldn't believe it. It must be the book, somehow he was subconsciously using mentalism to flirt with this beautiful woman. Or perhaps he just had a natural mesma stare. He knew he had to keep going.

'Well look,' he said. 'Maybe after the night is all done, we could have a quiet drink and you could... tell me... what... Hab... should be doing... or saying... as a DJ... for the club. For you. What can he do for you. What can I tell him... to do.. for you... for me... for you.'

'You want me to have a drink with you?' Bugger, she was on to him. He immediately started planning his escape from the conversation. He glanced over at the room and made sure he knew where the nearest door was and prepared to make an excuse to leave. Stephanie was still stood there, waiting for a reply. She hadn't said no. Rimmer was completely flummoxed by this.

'Um... um... um... well... yes.'

'Listen Rimmer, if you fix Hab so that he can introduce all of us correctly and stops doing whatever stand up routine has been programmed into him, I'll give you a whole lapdance for free.'

'Well.... I will get onto that,' Rimmer said. He pushed himself away from the bar and then slammed his hands down on to it, pretending it was a drum kit. He smiled and realised he had no idea what to do with his hands. 'Ugh... keep up the good work... leave it with me.'

She smiled at him and Rimmer walked off, trying his hardest not to cry with happiness. He was making it happen. Lister was just a huge bad luck charm, that's what it was. Now she was out of the way, he was going to be somebody.

The lowly, laughed at joke was going to turn into a big man. Or his name wasn't Reginald Mary Rimmer.

As soon as the last of the punters had left the ship, the girls were either back in their bunks or relaxing at the bar. Rimmer grabbed Holden, the technician on board the ship and headed down to the server room, which housed all of Hab's computers.

'A hard reboot? Rimmer, are you mental?' Holden said.

'I need it done, now. Rebooted and back to normal. Less wit and more... professionalism.'

Hab appeared on the screen in front of them. 'Alright, guys? What's this about a reboot? I'm working on multiple computations right now. I've got an engine breaking down, a drive plate that needs looking at and I have about ten one liners to come up with for tomorrow's set that absolutely need to be comedy zingers."

'You see?' Rimmer said. 'Turn him off and on again.'

'It's not as simple as that,' Holden said. 'You need to shut down each of his systems one by one, checking each part of the ship he's controlling as we go.'

'Well how long will that take?'

'A couple of hours?'

'No, I need it done now. I... I ... need it done.... now.' Stephaine was waiting for him upstairs in the club and Rimmer was desperate to show her Hab all back to normal.

'These subroutines you added for the DJ program have really screwed him up here, Rimmer,' Holden said, looking through a bunch of data on the screen in front of him.

'A quick off and on will sort him out. He's basically a glorified smart phone,' Rimmer said.

'Yeah, maybe,' Holden said. 'And maybe he'll turn back on even more messed up.'

'Fine, look, let's do the hard reboot. If it doesn't work, we'll do it again your way. Alright?'

'Whatever... you're the one telling me to do it.' He brought up a menu screen and pressed the restart button.

'Hold on guys,' Hab said. 'One of the engines....'

His face disappeared from the screen and the lights powered down in the room and were replaced by red emergency lighting and deafening alarms.

'What's going on?' Rimmer said, holding his hands to his ears.

'I don't know,' Holden said.


Three million years later, Pink Dwarf headed semi-aimlessly through deep deep space. Lister raced into the Pink Dwarf cockpit and sat in the pilot's chair. Rimmer ran in behind her and stared out of the front window.

'What is it Hab?' Rimmer said.

'It's another ship, Reginald,' Hab said, appearing on a screen next to him. 'Looks like it's been stranded for quite a while. Much like myself. I feel lonely... but then I remember I'm just a computer and I'm not supposed to feel lonely... which only makes it worse to be honest.'

'And Lister's going to try and dock with it?'

'That's the plan,' Lister said.

'This is never going to work. You're not even rated to fly a ship like this.'

'How do you know that, Rimmer?' Lister said. 'You don't know anything about me, not really. As far as you know, I could be an expert pilot.'

'Are you an expert pilot?'

'Nope. Never even seen the inside of a cockpit before.'

'It's illegal,' Rimmer said. 'And frankly... I'm not too comfortable with breaking the law, Lister.'

Lister sat back, took her hands off the pilot controls and looked up at Rimmer and his glowing H radiating from his forehead. 'Do you wanna do it?'

'I'm a hologram Lister... I can't touch anything.'

Lister took hold of the controls once more and slowly manoeuvred Pink Dwarf closer towards the larger ship ahead of them. 'It's the only way we can dock with the ship and get some upgrades for Hab's operating system.'

'He's fine,' Rimmer said. 'He's always been a bit quirky.'

'Rimmer,' Lister said. 'He can't even steer the ship properly. We hit a moon last week.'

'Ease off,' Hab said. 'It swerved straight towards me. There was no space to go around.'

'No space?' Lister said. 'We're in space. It's called space because there's lots of it.'

'What kind of ship is it, Hab?' Rimmer said.

'According to the readout, it's a Unicorp transport ship called the Venus Five. Twenty Fifth Century,' Hab said.

'Unicorp?' Rimmer said. 'The company that owned those supermarkets?'

'I guess they branched out over the years,' Hab said.

Cat slinked into the cockpit and started rubbing her groin against the navi-computer. 'Yeah, you like that? Huh, do ya...? Yeah you do!' Her choice of outfit today consisted of leopard print thigh high boots, black leather shorts and a crop top so small it seemed to act more like a bra than anything else. Rimmer was never sure how to act or feel around her. She looked absolutely stunning. Like a page three model, complete with gravity defying tits and athletic body. But there was something so animalistic about her that made him feel worried that he fancied the pants off her. Not that it mattered. He was dead. A hologram, brought to life by technology and a hard drive filled with his memories. He couldn't touch anything, feel anything. He had been determined to become a bigger, better Reginal Rimmer and somehow he had become less. He had given in. His whole life was a joke and now his death was one too. Typical. Rimmer scrunched his face up at her.

'That damn cat of yours is doing it again,' he said.

'I think she's in heat or something,' Lister said.

'She's always in heat.'

Rimmer watched Lister adjust the controls and move them closer to the Venus Five. The entire cockpit started vibrating and a terrible groaning noise filled the room.

'Oh god, we're all going to die,' Rimmer said.

'Where's reverse?' Lister said. She ran her hands across the control panel in front of her and found a lever. The huge ship in front of them was getting panic inducingly close as it pulled up, parallel to its side. 'Ah.'

Lister pushed forward on the lever and Pink Dwarf came to a sudden stop as the retro burners blasted out the front of the ship. Lister reached her left arm back over her seat and looked over her shoulder as their ship started reversing.

'You don't parallel park a spaceship, Lister!' Rimmer said. 'What are you even looking at?'

'What are you worried about? You're dead already.'

Pink Dwarf's reversing lights lit up and the ship slowly moved backwards into position along side the larger derelict Venus Five.


Rimmer stepped through the docking tube and up to the entrance of the Venus Five. He felt like the leader of an expedition party. Like the pioneers of interstellar space travel, who blasted off into infinity and were never heard from again. Rimmer and Lister were both from the 23$^{rd}$ Century; entering this ship would be like walking into the future for them. He was excited but took care not to let Lister and Cat see this. He wanted to put on a show of professionalism. He was their Captain now, though he knew they'd never call him that. Not yet. But if he were to act as such, just maybe he could become something more.

Lister and Cat walked up behind him, carrying flashlights.

'Are you sure we don't need spacesuits or something, Hab?' Lister said, looking at Hab's face on her watch.

'No Deb,' Hab said. 'All readings say the air inside is perfectly breathable. No life signs though.'

'Shiny,' Lister said. 'So anything we can get hold of is ours for the taking.'

'Oooh, men?' Cat said.

'No men,' Lister said. 'No lifesigns. Men tend to be living in one way or another.'

'Airlock opening now,' Hab said. The door in front of them hissed and slowly opened, revealing a dark room. Lister turned on her flashlight and stepped inside. Rimmer's red glow lit the place up with a pinkish hue and they looked around at the sleek space suits hanging in pods.

The door ahead of them opened and the three of them stepped through, into the main area of the mysterious ship.

# 2

'Oooh... new things,' Cat said. 'What's this? Shiny.' The three of them stood in a huge platform which overlooked the rest of the ship. Cat was looking up at the ceiling, where huge silver tubes plummeted down around them.

'Cat, don't touch anything,' Lister said.

'Do you think there's any way of getting the lights on, Hab?' Rimmer said.

'I can't figure out this interface, Reginald,' Hab said. 'The ship's computer is like nothing I've come across. Not that I spend my time coming across many things.'

Lister shined her flashlight around and saw a what looked like a keyboard. It was built in to a unit in the middle of the walkway and looked smooth and shiny.

'Look, a console,' Lister said. She knelt down next to it and rested her flashlight beside her, aiming it at the unit. She found a panel at the base and pulled out a knife from her lather jacket.

Rimmer walked over and added his red glow to the light from the flashlight and watched Lister wrench the panel off, revealing a bunch of wires and circuits.

'What are you doing?' Rimmer said.

'Hot-wiring the system,' Lister said.

'It's not a car, Lister.'

She pulled out a couple of wires and jammed them together, twisting the metal ends around one another. With a loud boom, the lights burst to life and a low hum started up around the console unit.

'Brutal,' Lister said. She got up and started tapping at the flat black screen at her waist. 'Umm... upgrades?'

'Upgrades,' the computer said. 'Select upgrades.'

'Voice activated?' Lister said. 'Nice.'

A holographic menu appeared above the console and listed all the different departments that upgrades were available for.

Rimmer looked out over the railings at the spectacle of the futuristic ship. It was incredible. The lights. The architecture. The design. He wondered if maybe they could simply move over to this ship and fly it back to Earth. It had to be faster than the bucket of rust and lube that was Pink Dwarf. He decided to explore. To seek out all he could about this new ship. The computer was voice activated. That meant he could ask it anything. Go anywhere. He'd learn all he could about this new ship and return to the others with an amazing plan and new found respect. He couldn't lose.

'Ok, I'm going to go have a look around,' Rimmer said.

'Yep, ok,' Lister said. 'Don't touch anything.'

Rimmer shot her a look back but she wasn't looking at him. She was too busy interacting with the computer, trying to find those upgrades for Hab. Essentially doing what was his job.

Cat started rubbing herself against the console unit. 'Oh this thing feels nice,' she said. 'All vibraty.'

Rimmer walked towards the giant escalator which had started moving when the power came on and made his way to the lower decks.

As he walked towards the doors of the large cargo bay they silently whizzed open. He looked at the doors feeling proud that the human race had eventually created space doors that didn't have to hiss at you every time you walked through them.

He looked around the large area, marvelling at the array of packaged food and water, all stored and safe for three million years. He moved on to the technology section and saw devices he couldn't even begin to fathom. Large pods. Small hand held devices. Any number of these items could be the key to getting back to their solar system.

Behind the shelves of shiny tech, Rimmer saw a female

head, sat on a shelf next to a few black glossy boxes and other pieces of electrical equipment. Her head had a shiny blue grey hue and her hair was pulled back tightly into a pony tail at the back.

He walked up to it and leaned over, amazed the workmanship. All their mechanoids had been walking metal and plastic but this one's skin looked real. It looked like it would be warm to the touch. He reached out with his hand, finger extended, shining his red glow onto it's skin. Rimmer pulled back, remembering his limitations as a hologram.

The head opened its eyes and stared at Rimmer, who jumped back with fright.

'Oh hi there,' she said. 'I haven't seen you around here before.'

'Um... no...' Rimmer said. 'Just arrived.'

'My name's Tyten. Very pleased to meet you.'

Rimmer stood up as tall as he could and introduced himself. 'Reginald Rimmer. Call me Regie... or Reg... or Bigman.'

Tyten smiled. 'I would shake your hand but it's all the way over there in that box.'

Rimmer looked around. Her body was in pieces, strewn around the surrounding shelves, hanging out of boxes in an annoyingly untidy way. He looked back at her. 'Have you been here for three million years?'

'Has it been three? Yes it must be about that now.'

'What have you been doing for three million years?'

'Well I've mostly been reading that fire exit sign over there.' About ten meters behind Rimmer was a door with a sign over the top which read *Fire Exit*. 'So much to learn from so few words.'

Rimmer bent over to look at the large box by the foot of the shelves. Inside was Tyten's chest piece. Her naked breasts looked practically perfect in every way.

'Oh my god,' Rimmer said. 'You're a sex robot.'

'I prefer the term… Stimulant.'

'The stimulants where I'm from were never this advanced. I bet you're programmed to do all sorts of kinky stuff.'

'Every pleasure ever discovered,' Tyten said. 'If you put my body together I'd be happy to show you.'

Rimmer smiled his widest smile which also meant flaring his nostrils. He felt his whole face stretch with sexual anticipation and then reality hit him like a wet fish. 'I'm a hologram,' he said. 'I can't touch anything.'

Tyten squinted her eyes and looked Rimmer up and down. 'Hmm, your light bee just needs upgrading.' She looked up at the ceiling. 'Upgrade option 52169.'

Rimmer also looked up and a laser beam shot down from above and hit Rimmer directly in the chest. He faded out, leaving behind his light bee, buzzing around like a confused fly. The lazer continued firing into the light be and soon the entire device was replaced with a bright glowing blue orb. The laser stops and Rimmer fades back into being once more. His red suit has changed to a brilliant blue.

'What just happened?' Rimmer said.

'I upgraded your light bee from soft light to hard light,' Tyten said.

'Hard light? I can touch? Oh my god... I can touch! Feel?'

'I am at your service.' Tyten licked her lips and smiled.

Rimmer excitedly walked over to her head and reached into his pants. For a moment he had hoped that it wasn't just his light bee that had been upgraded but upon pulling his cock out he discovered that was not the case. Thankfully the anticipation of actual sex with a female like being was enough to give him a quick hard light hard-on.

Tyten opened her mouth slightly and Rimmer slowly pushed his hard cock inside. 'Oh fuck yes. Oh yes.' The inside of her mouth felt warm and wet. Very different from the cold mechanical blowjob he was expecting. Tyten massaged his cock with her tongue and Rimmer's eyes widened as soon as she activated her vibrate function. "Oh now that's special," he said.

Rimmer grabbed hold of the shelves in front of him and pulled himself in and out of her mouth.

There was a knock to his left. He looked over and saw her right arm motioning with her fingers for him to come over.

'Ooh,' Rimmer said. He moves over a step or two and places his cock in between the blue fingers of the robot's artificial hand and they grasped his shaft firmly, stroking him up and down.

'That's what I'm talking about,' Rimmer said. 'Ok, I have got to put you together right now.'

'Are you any good with DIY jobs?' Tyten asked.

'Tyten… if there's one thing I'm an expert in… it's doing it myself.'


Lister and Cat looked at the holographic display of the computer console. There was a list of alternate computer personalities and appearances.

'Ooh,' Lister said. 'Not only can we upgrade Hab's systems, we can also give him a make over.'

Cat gave a tiny round of applause and jumped up and down with excitement.

'Option one,' Lister said. The simulation of Hab's face on the screen changed to that of a hunky male model with chiseled features.

'Give him bigger tits,' Cat said.

'Men don't have tits,' Lister said.

'But I like tits. I like your tits.' Cat nuzzled against Lister's chest and ran her hands all over them. Lister smiled and pushed them off.

'Ok, how about female.' The image transformed to a stern looking woman.

'A sexy female,' Cat said. The image changed once more into a gorgeous attractive woman. 'With reeeeeeeally big tits.' The image's breasts started growing to a huge size until they were twice as big as her head. 'Well, I'm happy.'

'I'm not sure Hab will be,' Lister said. 'Cancel image update.' The image warps back to Hab's original appearance.

'No,' Cat said. 'I liked the one with the big boobs.'

'We can't give Hab boobs. We just need the upgraded firmware. Download to the Pink Dwarf.'

'Download commencing,' the computer said. 'Estimated download time… 20 minutes.'

'Smeg,' Lister said. 'Futuristic spaceship with dial up download speed.' She started making her way back towards Pink Dwarf. 'Come on Cat.'

'Can we eat now?' she asked.

'What do you wanna eat?'

'Pussay!'

Lister smiled and looked over the railings at the levels below them. 'Yo, Rimmer? You coming?'

Rimmer twisted on Tyten's head to her chest piece and looked back at the door to the cargo area. 'Um, I will be... give me a few minutes.'

Tyten opened her eyes and Rimmer took a step back marveling at his handy work. His cock was still rock solid, which frankly surprised him. He put it down to his new hard light projection tech and happily pulled out his cock once more.

'You're sure this is ok?' he said.

'I am made for pleasure,' Tyten said. She stood up and Rimmer took in her incredible design. In pieces she was beautiful but put together she was a knockout. She had the perfect body, a waist so tight but a generous bum and boobs.

She reached out and grabbed Rimmer, pulling him towards her. She took hold of his cock with her hand and started caressing it gently. He could feel his cock get wet and he looked down to see lubricant oozing out of her palm.

'Now, that is handy,' he said.

She got to her knees and cradled his holographic balls in her hand and increased the speed of her other hand. Rimmer's mouth was agape; he had never felt anything like this. He wasn't sure what to say or what noise to make but he had to say something. He was worried it would come out as a scream or yelp but as Tyten continued to masturbate his cock so incredibly fast and the whirs of pistons and electric motors radiated from her arm he simply just blurted out exactly what he was thinking. 'Oh my god, thank you so much... this is the best bloody day of my entire life... and death, thank you, thank you, thank you, thank you!'

'You're most welcome... Bigman.' She pulled her hand

away and thrust her face onto his cock, taking the entire shaft down her throat. Rimmer gasped and made a small squeak as she pushed her forehead against his stomach and started licking his balls. Her tongue was smooth and so incredibly agile. It tickled every part of his scrotum, exploring his entire nether region with a slippery lick. Tyten slowly pulled her head away, releasing his swollen cock from her throat. She looked up at his quivering face. 'What do you like?'

'Um... honestly... anything...' Rimmer said.

Tyten lifted her hand to her face and spat on two of her fingers and moved them under Rimmer's balls and pushed them against his arse.

Rimmer jolted backwards. 'Ooh, maybe not that. When I said anything... I really meant... just sex is fine... nothing kinky... yet... I understand that some people may want something a little extra in the bedroom department but honestly all I really want and need... is just your basic sexy sex type stuff. You know... sex.'

'I'm programmed to serve,' Tyten said and stood up once more, turned around and bent over the large plastic box her chest was packed in. She stuck her arse cheeks out at Rimmer and waved her buttocks at him, enticing him over. 'I want you inside me. I have five vibrate levels and sixteen levels of moistness, I can squirt if you want. I also have three orgasm difficulty modes if you're interested in trying your luck?'

Rimmer positioned himself behind her and gently put his hands on her buttocks. They were soft, squishy, yet firm. It was like nothing he'd ever felt before... literally. 'I don't suppose you have a demo function do you?' Rimmer pushed his hard cock inside her wet robo pussy. He was curious if she was going to be oozing WD40. The smell was very pleasant. A summery freshness with a hint of strawberry. He took in the fragrance through his ever flaring nostrils and pushed harder into Tyten who, amusingly, also began to tighten. Around his cock. 'This really does feel quite satisfying, Tyten.'

'I'm glad. Should I turn on my vibrate function now?'

'Sure, why not,' Rimmer said with a smirk. He couldn't believe it, he was actually doing it. Sure, it was with a robotic prostitute but it still counted. As Tyten's pussy began to gently vibrate around his cock, Rimmer took a few moments to marvel at his new body. He could feel more; everything was more sensitive. His soft light body fed him information of what things might feel like. Everything seemed off. Plastic felt too metallic. Water felt like custard. And sitting down felt like he was in a bath. It was odd but he was slowly growing accustomed to it. His upgrades meant he could sense everything how it should be. Not that he was totally aware what shagging a sexbot should feel like but if he was to guess, he would have said it should feel exactly like what he was feeling right now.

Tyten pushed back against his hard cock, slapping her buttocks against his stomach. She started moaning out loud.

'What?' Rimmer said. 'What have I done wrong?'

'Nothing,' Tyten said. 'You're making me come.'

'Right... of course... yes.' He was proud. He had made someone orgasm. He felt like he was playing a computer game and had finally unlocked some kind of achievement. As he pummeled away at the back of her, he wondered what else she may do if he did it harder. Rimmer placed his hands on Tyten's hips and thrust forwards into her pussy harder and harder.

Tyten responded with yelp after yelp, followed by a huge scream. She gripped the plastic box hard and managed to crush the edge with her powerful hand. Her pussy continued to get wetter and wetter and with a huge contraction of her pussy, Rimmer's cock was thrust out of her, quickly followed by a gush of warm liquid.

It hit Rimmer square in the groin and he looked down, slightly annoyed to see her ejaculate covering his new blue suit. The liquid, however, simply dripped off the glowing suit. It seemed to be indestructible and unsoilable. He felt his erection harden even more at the thought of it and turned his attention back to the gushing fluids, streaming out of Tyten's pussy. She was now showing off with a flurry of energetic bursts of liquid, creating fancy fountains which sprayed down over the room. Rimmer clapped his hands together and smiled. 'Marvellous.'

Tyten turned back around and sat on the box, lifting her legs high into the air. Rimmer looked down at her perfectly designed pussy. She was hairless and swollen down there. Pushing his cock back into her felt like he was placing it into warm fresh bread. It wasn't even a simile. Rimmer knew for a fact what his penis in warm fresh bread felt like. His own mother once caught him buggering half a cheese and ham baguette when they were on holiday in the Algarve. They exchanged looks and never spoke about it ever.

Rimmer could feel his erection dwindling and realised this particular moment was not the right time to be reminiscing about his mother catching him in the middle of lewd acts. He tried to focus on the moment in hand. He was having sex with a robotic woman with incredible tits and he needed to stay hard. He knew Lister and Cat would only laugh at him if he failed to have sex with a machine designed for having sex with losers like him.

Tyten seemed to notice the change in his cock and looked up at Rimmer. She raised one hand squeezed his nipple. Hard.

Rimmer suddenly felt a release of adrenaline and responded by squeezing her right breast. Hard.

Tyten took her other hand and pushed it under her bum and gripped Rimmer's bollocks. She gently cupped them and Rimmer pushed his cock harder into Tyten's pussy.

Rimmer was now feeling sensations from every part of his body. His nipple. His penis. His testicles. Even his left shin felt good. And that never happened. Tyten obviously knew exactly what she was doing. He felt her hand on his balls loosen and explore underneath to his arse. Her fingers pressed around his arsehole and Rimmer was about to ask her politely to stop but as she teased her lubricated fingers inside him his eyes widened and his cock pulsated with pleasure. It was like she found a trigger. She gently stroked the inside of his arsehole and Rimmer hunched forward, pushing his cock deeper into her and letting out a cry of happiness as he shot his hot load inside her. At least he assumed he had. He wasn't sure exactly what was coming out of him. He pulled himself out of her in time to see a jet of bright white holographic semen fly out of his cock and land on her stomach and breasts and slowly disappear.

'Geronimo,' Rimmer said.

Tyten sat up, took hold of his cock and licked up the shaft and around the head as if she was cleaning him up. 'Was it pleasurable, Reginald?' she said.

'Absolutely, yes. The best I've ever had actually. Maybe we could do this again?'

'It would be my pleasure.'

Rimmer pulled up his holographic pants and trousers and smiled to himself. It was a sign. He was finally going places. And to top it off he had found himself someone who would allow him to have sex with them. It was like having a girlfriend without any of those annoying drawbacks that come with them. Things like talking. Conversation. Having to buy them things or like them.


Lister and Cat sat in front of a computer monitor in the mid-section. A small notification blipped on the screen letting them know the download was complete.

'Ok Hab,' Lister said. 'Looks like this upgrade is all ready for you.'

Hab appeared on the screen. His craggy face didn't seem interested at all. If anything, it seemed insulted. 'Ok, restarting now.'

Hab shut himself down and a few lights went out around them. Emergency lighting activated and Rimmer walked into the room in his shiny new blue suit.

'Ahh, what a wonderful day it's been,' he said.

Lister stood up and walked over to him. 'Rimmer, what happened to you?'

'Upgrades. My new hard light body thanks to my new friend here." He raised his arm towards the door and Tyten walked in. 'I'd like to introduce you all to Tyten. She's a sexbot.'

'Hello,' Tyten said. 'I am at your service.'

'She does sex,' Rimmer said. 'Sex. With me.'

'Sounds like hell,' Cat said, filing her nails.

The lights flickered and came back on to full capacity and a woman with large breasts filled the monitor where Hab was.

'Hi, wanna chat?' the woman said. 'I just need your credit card details. I really want to talk with you. I'll show you everything.'

'Boobs,' Cat said. She got to her feet and stared up at the screen.

'Oh my god,' Rimmer said. 'You utter morons. You've downloaded a pop-up ad.'

'Hab?' Lister said. 'Oh smeg, can we delete it?'

Hab's floating head appeared next to the woman and bobbed around, looking truly excited. 'Bugger that. It's been three million years since I've had any company. I bet she gives great head.' He started rubbing his head on her boobs, pushing his scalp in between her cleavage. He slowly made his way down to her pussy and started rubbing his nose on her. 'Oh yeah, you like that don't you!'

An alarm sounded and red lights started flashing around the entire mid-section.

'Hab,' Lister said. 'Get your face out of her tits. What is that?'

'Hmm, oh, it's a distress signal,' Hab said momentarily moving from between the woman's legs on his screen.

'A distress signal from who?' Lister said.

'Aliens,' Rimmer said. He marched up to the video monitor. 'Hab, leave the woman alone and show us what this signal is.'

The pop-up ad faded away and Hab turned his attention to the signal. 'It's from a Space Corps escape pod.'

'So not aliens then?' Rimmer said.

'No,' Hab said. 'Seems like it's coming from inside that small nebula up ahead.'

'How long until we reach it, Hab?' Lister said.

'Should be about two weeks at out current speed.'

'Any details about who's inside?' Rimmer said.

'There seems to be a transmission of some kind but it's too faint to make out at the moment. Details within the distress signal state that it's a Space Corps pod, containing one Officer Christopher Kochanski.'

'A man?' Cat said.

Lister looked over at her, equalling her excitement. 'A bloody fucking, smegging real life man. Hab, we're heading for that signal.'

'Sure,' Hab said. 'Looks like we're all getting lucky this trip.'

# BYTE III
# BACKWARDS BANGING

# 1

'Five minutes until we're in tractor beam range,' Lister said. She was sat in the cockpit of Pink Dwarf, staring at the monitor in front of her. Over the past few weeks she had got pretty good at flying the enormous spaceship. She didn't know what the fuss was about to be honest. There wasn't much to do when it came to flying a ship through space. You went forward. That was it. There mostly nothing to go around. Sure, parking and landing and all that stuff was a bit of a hassle but mostly it was just a lot of sitting in the cockpit, staring out of the view screen as the ship went forwards very fast. Even going very fast seemed a bit underwhelming. When you didn't have anything to relate your speed to, going a steady 100,000 miles an hour felt pretty much the same as going 5,000 miles an hour. Even the acceleration wasn't felt due to the intertial dampners.

Tyten sat in the co-pilot's chair and tapped a button on her screen. An image of the predicted location of the Space Corps Escape Pod appeared on the main viewing screen. 'This must be exciting for you Miss Lister,' Tyten said in her breathy voice. 'The possibility of a man to have sex with must be overwhelming.'

Lister looked over at her, feeling like she'd just been called a slut. 'He may not even be my type,' she said.

'Oh, of course he will, Miss Lister. Reginald made it perfectly clear to me what your ideal sexual partner was.'

'Oh yeah? And what exactly is my ideal sex partner?'

'Reginald said as long as they're breathing and find you attractive, you'd be more than happy to have them inside you.'

'Tyten, you can't say that.'

'Was Reginald mistaken in his description?'

That's what annoyed her the most. It was a pretty damn accurate description. Over the years she'd made a pretty dollar-pound or two shagging anyone and everyone that had the money to spend. She wasn't phased by it. She didn't care. She had been able to buy the most luxurious clothes. The most expensive jewellery. She had the best bunk room on the ship. Filled with the best Artificial Reality games that money could buy. Life had been pretty damn good. She was on course to retiring from the space stripper game when she was thirty. She had plans to invest her money in a ship of her own and offer cruises across the solar system. She could sit back and have her cabin boys and girls fulfil all her needs and the passengers would pay for it. Captain Deb Lister. It had a ring to it. Of course, that was three million years ago. Without a Mimas bank nearby she couldn't access any of her savings. There was nothing to spend it on anyway.

'Yes, he was mistaken,' Lister said. 'Why do you hang around with him so much anyway?'

'He enjoys the sex,' Tyten said. 'He uses me every day. Twice on Saturdays.'

'I know that, we all hear it.'

'He likes it when I orgasm loudly.'

'But do you like it?'

'It's not important what I like. If Reginald is happy with the sex I provide him with, then I'm happy.'

'Ugh, you know back in my time we had androids like you. Not quite as... sophisticated... but we had sexbots. They were mindless. Drones that guys ploughed away into night after night. They didn't have brains. Just a few sentences that could be programmed in. But you think, right?'

'Yes, I think. I can help around the home. I can cook and clean. But what I'm really good at is sex.'

'Yeh, I know that. Let me ask you this... can you learn stuff?'

Tyten cocked her head slightly. 'I can learn knew sexual positions if that's what you mean?'

'No, that's not what I mean. Tyten... if there were no men on board. No-one who wanted sex... what would you do?'

Tyten cocked her head again. 'Well, I'm not sure. There's always been someone who wanted sex. I suppose... I might try... painting.'

'Painting?'

'Yes Miss Lister. I've seen images of artwork by a great number of artists and I've always wondered if I could also create something... artistic.'

'There ya go, do that. Next time Reginald beckons you for some lovemaking, tell him your busy painting.'

'But then he wouldn't be having sex with me?'

'Tyten? If you had a choice, would you rather be fucking Rimmer or creating an artistic masterpiece?'

'I've never had a choice before.'

'Well you've got one now,' Lister said. 'Remember that.'

An alarm sounded. Hab appeared on the monitor to the side of the cockpit. 'Coming up to tractor beam distance now Deb.'

'Thanks Hab,' Lister said and turned her attention back to the view screen in front of her.

'Want me to slow the ship down or did you want to keep it in Manual?' Had said.

'Keep in manual,' Lister said. 'I want to learn how to do this.'

Rimmer walked in and saw Lister at the helm. 'Um, Lister. What are you doing?'

'We're in Tractor beam range of the stasis pod. I'm slowing us down so we can bring it in.'

'I mean, what are you doing piloting Pink Dwarf. That's what Hab is for.'

'We don't know how long we're gonna be out here, Rimmer. What if he breaks down? Goes space crazy?'

'Oh, you're the back up are you?'

'I'm doin' good.' Lister pressed more buttons and held the pilot controls tightly. 'Ok, activate tractor beam, Tyten.'

Tyten presses a few buttons. 'Tractor beam activated,'

she said.

'Um, Tyten doesn't have to do that,' Rimmer said.

Lister scowled at him. 'I suppose she should be in the back sucking you off, right?'

'It's not my fault she enjoys my naked company.'

'Miss Lister,' Tyten said. 'What do we do about the giant swirly space thing?'

Lister looked out and saw an enormous swirly space thing. 'Holy shit, Hab, what is that?'

'It's a worm hole, Deb,' Hab said. 'Your basic tear in the fabric of space and time. Probably best to avoid it.'

'Ok, retros on full,' Lister said. The whole ship vibrated and shook and then suddenly everything was still and silent and dark. All the lights went off. Hab was gone from the screen. The entire cockpit had been plunged into darkness. 'Frak, I've lost control,' Lister said.

'Nothing seems to be working,' Tyten said.

'What the hell happened,' Rimmer said.

A soft buzzing sound answered his question. All three of them stepped out of the cockpit and into the mid-section where they saw Cat lying on the ground with a vibrating wand pushed against her pussy. The wand was plugged into a socket near the entrance to the cockpit and a small black, important looking plug was lying on the floor.

'Cat, what the hell are you doing?' Lister said.

'I'm getting my love on,' Cat said. She pushed the wand harder onto her wet pussy and groaned loudly as she increased the power. 'Oh my god, this thing is powerful... I think I'm gonna squirt.'

'You just unplugged the entire cockpit.'

'I wanted to be near you guys.'

Rimmer put his hands on his hips and stepped towards her. 'Listen you deranged moggy. We are trying to prevent a stasis pod from flying into a worm hole.'

'So?' Cat said, continuing to pleasure herself.

Lister crouched down next to her. 'So, there could be a survivor in there.'

'So?'

Rimmer frowned. 'So, if we get sucked into it, there's no

telling where we'd end up.'

Cat increased the power of her vibrator to maximum and smiled. 'I really don't see what this has to do with my special time.'

'Unplug your vibrator and go use another socket,' Lister said.

Cat looked up at Lister. 'Fine, but this corner right here… is all mine.' She pulled the vibrator away from her pussy and let out an almighty scream as a gush of liquid sprayed from between her legs and rained down over the floor, the wall and Rimmer.

'We have got to teach her about labels,' Rimmer said, wiping the dripping fluid from his face.

Cat put the black plug back into the socket and the cockpit powered up again. Rimmer and Lister ran back in and stared at the worm hole which grown double in size.

'Hab, are we still on target?' Lister said.

'Tractor beam re-activated,' Hab said. 'We've got it but the worm hole is pulling us in.'

'Deactivate the tractor beam, Hab,' Rimmer said.

'No, we can pull it back,' Lister said. 'Let's turn us around.' She pushed a few buttons and pulled hard to the left on the controls.

Pink Dwarf slowly turned around as it hurled towards the worm hole. The thrusters at the back went to full burn but still it headed towards the giant swirly space thing.

'The gravity is too strong, I'm afraid Deb,' Hab said.

'We are going to either get crushed into an infinitely small space or spat out an infinite distance away,' Rimmer said.

'Alright, deactivate the tractor beam, Hab.'

A pair of black shades appeared on Hab's face. 'It's too late now,' he said. 'We're being dragged in. No way to stop it. May as well enjoy the ride. Surfs up Big Kahuna!'

Lister grabbed hold of the pilot's chair and hauled herself into it. 'Strap yourselves in guys,' she said.

Tyten sat in the co-pilot chair and she and Lister buckled their seat belts. Rimmer lunged for the navigation chair and the entire ship started spinning around, throwing Rimmer against the wall.

'Inertial dampness are offline,' Lister yelled.

'I know,' said Rimmer as he was hurled across the cockpit again and slammed into the other side of the room.

Pink Dwarf spun around inside the worm hole, still holding the stasis pod in its tractor beam in front of it. Slowly it pulled it closer and the pod entered the ship's belly just as a tunnel of flashing lights opened up and sucked Pink Dwarf through it and lightning speed and suddenly spat it back out into empty space, arse first.

The ship hurtled backwards through space and towards a giant asteroid, where it skimmed the surface and crash landed. The ship slowly came to a halt. The engines fizzled out and everything was still.

Lister, Rimmer, Cat and Tyten all stood around the stasis pod in the mid-section, which had been brought up by the skutters. The room was a mess; equipment was strewn all over the place and bits of metal, plastic and liquid covered the floor.

Hab appeared on the view screen. 'Ffo ekat ot elba eb dluohs ew, moor ograc eht ot nwod dop sisats eht dnes ew fi,' he said.

Rimmer sighed. 'Oh Jesus, he's still doing it. What if we hit him on the side really hard?'

Lister looked down at the pod and the small printed name on the front. 'Christopher Kochanski. I bet he's cute.'

Cat kicked the pod. 'I don't get why it wont open, though.'

Lister entered the open code again. 'This is definitely the space corps emergency open code. Everyone's taught it.' She rubbed her eye. It was swollen and red. 'My damn eye. Don't know where this redness has come from. And my butt cheeks hurt.' She pulled down her leather jeans and revealed a red hand print on her right buttock.

Cat saw it and pointed. 'Hey, you've got a rash in the shape of a hand, that's cool!'

'Ruoh na flah tsap eht rof uoy gnillet neeb ev'i tahw s'taht,' Hab said.

Rimmer picked up an empty mug from the floor and looked inside. 'Is it just me, or is the whole backwards talking making you think that maybe this worm hole spat us out in a parallel universe where time runs a little different?'

'Are you suggesting time is running backwards here?' Lister said.

Rimmer held the mug upside down and boiling hot coffee poured upwards from the ground into the mug until it was full. 'All I'm saying is… that's not normal.'

# 2

Rimmer placed the mug of steaming hot coffee into place under the drinks dispenser and watched as the steaming brown liquid jetted upwards from the mug. 'Try it,' he said. 'Push in the lock code for the stasis pod... but in reverse.'

Lister reached for the keypad once more and the entire pod hissed and the metal hatch on top slowly opened. Lister keyed in the lock code in reverse. A dense white fog hung in the air around the opened hatch.

Hab's screen fizzled and his image reappeared. 'That's better... in this universe effect precedes cause.'

Lister looked up at him. 'Things are going to happen before something makes them happen?'

'Exactly,' he said.

Kochanski sat up in the pod and opened his eyes. He looked around at the odd looking characters around him. 'Where am I?' he said.

Rimmer put his fists on his hips, smiled at him and said, 'Stranded on an asteroid in a backwards dimension, three million years from Earth... if you want to get technical.'

Kochanski locked eyes with Lister. 'Hi,' he said.

'Hi,' she said. He was a handsome man with a toned body. He was wearing Space Corps issue white underwear and his skin looked shiny. He was sweaty and smelled musky.

Kochanski smiled and held out his hand. 'I'm Kochanski... Chris.'

Lister shook it. 'Um… Lister… Deb'

He looked at her face and squinted. 'Are you ok? Your face…'

'Yeah, it's my eye.' She put her finger to it and felt a strange moist liquid around it. 'I think it's getting filled with pus.' She moved her hand around her face and felt more of the strange sticky liquid. 'Oh… my face… it's all sticky… what the hell is this?'

Kochanki pulled himself out of the pod and stood up. 'Is it warm in here?' he said. 'I feel like I'm burning up.'

'No, it's not,' Rimmer said. 'What is wrong with you two? You're all sweaty.'

Lister looked down at her body and felt her chest. She was sweaty too. What the hell was going on? She pulled off her top, revealing her large boobs in a black bra. 'It is hot… it's really hot.' She pulled down her leather jeans and started hopping about, pulling off her boots.

Rimmer looked astonished. 'Yes, let's just strip off in front of complete strangers. Stick to what you're good at eh Listy?'

Lister continued to pull her jeans off, quickly followed by her bra and underwear until she was completely naked.

'Jesus,' Kochanski said. 'I think I need to do the same.' He pulled down his white boxers exposing his swollen cock.

'What the smeg are you guys doing?' Rimmer said.

'Oh god,' Lister said. 'It's backwards! It's all backwards!'

'What's backwards?' Kochanski said.

Lister dropped to her knees in front of him. Kochanski grabbed his cock, which rapidly became fully erect.

'Oh jesus,' he said. 'What the hell is happening?'

The sticky liquid on Lister's face was suddenly catapulted off her skin and flew through the air and into the end of Kochanski's cock.

Cat beamed a huge smile and started applauding. 'This is like the greatest circus ever.'

'This is unbelievable,' Rimmer said. 'They just met.'

'Well technically, in this universe they're about to never see each other again,' Hab said.

'Ugh, let's go figure out what's wrong with the engines.'

Rimmer walked out looking incredibly jealous that someone else, other than him was having sex on the ship. Tyten and Cat followed him and left Lister and Kochanski to it.

Lister sat on the edge of the stasis pod and opened her legs, leaning back slightly.

Kochanski started dancing around, hoping from one leg to another, grabbing his cock tightly. 'Oh my god,' he said. I'm gonna come... I'm gonna come.' He knelt down beside Lister and pushed his hard cock inside her and started pummeling her pussy hard. 'Wait... no I'm not... this is too weird.'

It took a minute to get used to having sex backwards but Lister quickly learned that if she were to scream out loudly, Kochanski would push his cock deep inside her, then pull back quickly. A wave of orgasmic ecstasy would flow over her and slowly dissipate and then Kochanski would fuck her really hard and fast for a few seconds. Just like Hab said, effect preceded cause. This hot sweaty man was undoing her orgasms. It was an odd sensation but still pleasurable.

Lister's nipple began to ache as she felt the cock push in and out of her wet pussy. Kochanski reached over and grabbed her boobs and started caressing it. The sensation got even stronger and her nipple was pulsing with pain. It became too much to bear. Lister was about to scream out in pain... but she realised that wouldn't give her what she needed. She needed the pain gone... and this universe was backwards but all of them were still thinking forwards.

'Squeeze my nipple,' she said. 'Quick!'

Kochanski let go of her breast and squeezed her nipple hard. The pain quickly disappeared. She looked at Kochanski, sweat was dripping upwards from her chest and stomach up to his forehead. His face was glowing and his hair was a mess.

Lister smiled and put her hand on his chest to push him away but instead, he was rapidly forced down towards her face and they started kissing. She ran her fingers through his hair and saw that it became less messy the more she did it. He pulled his cock out of her and Lister got up and turned around. She moved towards the navigation desk at the rear of the room and bent over it. Kochanski followed her, grabbed hold of her waist and slowly pushed himself inside her.

As he continued to fuck her she felt her buttock start to ache. The pain grew and grew and she quickly realised where that hand shaped mark on her came from. She could also tell exactly when he was going to unslap her. She closed her eyes and waited for it. Kochanski moved his hand from her waist and gently placed it on her buttock. There was a loud slapping sound and he quickly tore his hand away from her skin and a rapid speed. The red hand print was gone. After another couple of minutes of fucking Lister felt Kochanski's hand on her back and a ton of electrical equipment that was lying around the floor, sprang into the air and slid onto the table. Lister lurched backwards as the equipment collided with her body and Kochanski seemed to gently collapse to the ground and Lister squatted on him.

It made her wonder how dates in this universe worked. Especially one night stands. Two strangers awkwardly meet and act all awkward around each other as they get undressed, get into bed and fall asleep. When they wake up in the middle of the night they feel excited and relaxed and then start fucking each other until they're feeling all awkward again. They then proceed to chat and drink until they no longer know each other and leave to go their separate ways.

Lister wondered what would happen if they were stuck here for a while. She had to think backwards. Why were they fucking? Are they boyfriend and girlfriend? It didn't seem like that kind of sex. It felt like the first time. Was Rimmer right? Was she just a slut who'd fuck anything? It felt so good though. And Chris Kochanski was a very handsome man. He knew what he was doing. She decided not to dwell on it and just let whatever unhappened to unhappen. Life was easier that way.

They continued to unfuck each other around the room until the mid-section looked a lot more tidy. Lister noticed Kochanski's face looking incredibly wet. Droplets of liquid were flying from the ground, up to his face. She quickly laid down on the floor and felt her knees go wobbly. Her legs were twitching and she suddenly felt the rush of an enormous orgasm hit her hard. Kochanski staggered around, placing more and more liquid on his face with his hands. He then got to his knees and managed to spray a whole load of female ejaculate off his face and into her pussy. Lister unscreamed an almighty orgasm and it soon disappeared all together as Kochanski rammed his fingers inside her and proceeded to unfingerfuck her. The sweatiness had slowly left her body and Kochanski's hair was now immaculate. They got off the floor and Lister got to her knees and started unsucking his cock. He staggered backwards slightly and stepped into his white underwear, which Lister grabbed hold of and pulled up his trouser legs. She could feel his cock getting softer and softer in her mouth. She pulled away and stood up. Her underwear flew across the room and landed right in Kochanski's hand. He looked at it amazed and got to his knees and put them on Lister and pulled them up her legs. Lister held out her arm and her bra flew into her hand. She put it back on and proceeded to dress herself whilst kissing Kochanski. They're hands were all over each other. And then quite suddenly... they stopped and stepped backwards from each other and smiled.

'We just fucked in reverse,' Lister said.

'I feel incredibly horny,' Kochanski said. 'Sex in this universe feels very unsatisfying.'

'At least you don't feel sticky and sweaty afterwards.'

Rimmer walked back into the Mid-section. 'Well, now that you're both done... maybe we can get out of here?'

'I thought we were stuck,' Lister said.

'If you think backwards, it all makes sense. Tell 'em Hab.'

Hab appeared on the screen. 'Just like how you opened Kochanski's pod by entering the lock code. We should be able to take off by slamming on the brakes as it were.'

'So if you'd like to get into the cockpit, we try returning to our own universe,' Rimmer said.

'I think we may need more time,' Tyten said. She was was the door way and holding a large canvas painting.

'What's that?' Rimmer said.

Cat ran up behind Tyten and looked at the painting and

started laughing hard. 'We found it, in the living quarters. Just standing there on an easel.'

'A painting,' said Lister. 'Why does that mean we can't take off? Or Land?'

'Because,' said Tyten. 'I think I have to unpaint it first.' She turned the canvas around and showed it to Rimmer, Lister and Kochanski. They were impressed.

Lister cocked her head to one side and nodded. 'Not a bad likeness. Really great work Tyten.'

'What the smeg is that?' Rimmer said.

The painting was of Reginald A. Rimmer fucking a toaster with his tiny penis with a speech bubble which had him saying, *Call me Bigman*.

# 3

Tyten placed the canvas back on its easel and stared at it. Rimmer stood next to her and watched as she picked up the paint brush from the small tray at the bottom.

'And why exactly did you paint this?' Rimmer said.

'I really have no idea, Reginald,' Tyten said. 'I suppose if I unpaint it, we'll find out what caused me to portray you in such a way.'

'Yes, unpaint it... quick as you like.' He sneered at her and walked away.

Tyten held the brush up to the canvas and gently stroked the surface. Paint disappeared with every movement and she began to unpaint it. She felt proud she had painted it. The quality was pretty good and she had definitely managed to capture Reginald's likeness. She knew he was unhappy with the context and she couldn't quite begin to imagine what would have made her do it. The purpose of the painting seemed to be to upset him. Tyten was well aware of humans tendency towards passionate feelings of emotions. Anger, envy, jealousy... but she had never experienced them. She ran through some situations in her mind which may have caused her to embarrass Reginald in that way.

Perhaps if he were to have told her she was terrible at sex? No, he would never say that. For one, she was incredible at sex and second Reginald seemed like the kind of man who would beg for it. She continued to unpaint her personal masterpiece and thought about what Miss Lister had told her. She had a choice. If she'd rather paint, she could. Did she really enjoy sucking Reginald's cock? Or was it simply in her programming. If you automatically smile every time someone sticks their cock inside you, does that mean you're really enjoying it? She'd never thought about these things before.

Rimmer walked into the cockpit where Lister and Kochanski were making preparations to leave.

'This is your doing, isn't it,' Rimmer said.

'How is it my fault?'

'You said something to her. Somehow managed to get her seeing me the way you do.'

'And how's that?'

Rimmer scowled at her. 'You know what I mean.'

'Look, all I said was that she had a choice.'

'Why?' Rimmer said. 'Why would you tell her that?'

'Because it's true. You can't just force her to have sex with you.'

'She's a sexbot, Lister... that's kind of the point.'

'Well not any more. She's part of the crew now and that means that she's got a choice about who she fucks.'

'Fine,' he said and turned around and stormed out of the cockpit.

Kochanski turned to Lister, looking astonished. 'Wow, he really wants to have sex.'

'Yeah, it's a shame he's such a prick because he's not exactly bad looking.'

'What? Are you saying you'd fuck him?'

'Hell no... he'd have to have better hair. Be incredibly charismatic, a deeper voice... and his dick would have to be a lot bigger than it was in that painting!'

Kochanski smiled and looked at her. Lister smiled and turned her attention to the controls. Hab had told them to set everything up as though they had just crash landed. She felt an incredible amount of pressure suddenly. It was the way he was looking at her. As far as she knew, they were the last two humans in the universe. At some point they were going to have that conversation... about keeping the race alive. Having babies. But what about the next generation? Do they just end up all incestuous? The human race would end up looking like people from Norfolk. Maybe she should get the talk out of the way, she figured.

'Look, I wanted to say something,' Lister said.

'Something about us suddenly having sex the moment we met, like it was destiny?'

'Yeah, something about that.'

'It's ok... I don't believe in destiny or fate. Not in our universe anyway. Whatever happens, happens. We're in control of our future, right?'

'I like the sound of that,' Lister said and smiled again. She continued flipping switches and programming settings to match those as if they had just landed.

Tyten danced her brush across the canvas one last time and took the last stroke of paint off it. She felt sad that the picture had gone but instead of feeling like she had removed the image she looked at the canvas as having the potential of the image. In this universe it was destined to become a picture of Reginald copulating with a toaster. She still felt like she had done something very wrong though and decided to show Reginald that the painting had gone. She picked up the canvas and took it out of the bunk room and through towards the midsection where she saw him talking to Hab.

Hab rolled his eyes. 'Wipe Tyten's memory?'

'Yes, you floating imbecile. Can you do it or not?'

'She's from the 25th Century Reginald. I can't just hack into her positronic brain and wipe it. Maybe if you get her close to an electro magnet?'

'Ok, are you being sarcastic or would that actually make her forget she had that little conversation with Lister?'

Tyten stepped into the mid-section. 'Well, I think I now understand why I painted that picture.'

'Tyten, no no, you misunderstood, I was merely trying to get you back to normal, is all.'

'What if I don't want to be a sexbot?'

'That's fine, all I'm saying is... maybe just ease into it... ween yourself off sex. How about we head inot the bunk room and...'

'I think I'd rather stick my genitals in a toaster, Reginald.' Tyten turned and walked out, feeling a sensation she had never felt before. It was pride. She felt alive. She couldn't believe she turned down sex. It was unbelievable.

Lister yelled out from the cockpit, 'Ok guys, strap yourselves in, I think we're ready to crash land.'

Rimmer and Tyten made their way to the cockpit and sat down. Cat strolled in, yawned and looked at everyone panicking to get their seat belts fastened.

'Cat, sit down and strap in or you may get hurt,' Lister said.

'How? In this place if I got hurt during the crash I'd already be hurt, right?'

Lister shook her head, this universe was confusing. 'Ok, hang on. Firing retros.' The retros engines, which were used to brake the ship ignited just before Lister pushed the button to stop them. The ship rocked from side to side and suddenly pelted backwards across the surface of the huge asteroid.

The breaking rockets stopped firing and Lister immediately activated them. She couldn't help but think that crashing in reverse took a lot more concentration than forwards. 'Now slowly increasing thrusters up to full... and plotting a course for that asteroid. Are we all sure this makes sense?'

'If you think about it it makes perfect sense,' Tyten said. 'In this universe we crash land on an asteroid and I overhear Reginald plotting to erase my memory. I get angry at him for this and so paint an embarrassing painting of him making love to a toaster with his tiny penis. You and Mr Kochanski flirt for a while and then get it on in the mid-section. He jizzes in your eye, so you lock him in the stasis pod. We take off and you jettison him into outer space using the tractor beam. You see? Perfect sense.'

Kochanski looked over to Lister. 'I guess this means we'd better get to know each other.'

'I guess so,' Lister said.

'Ugh,' Rimmer said. 'Barf city.'

Pink Dwarf flew backwards through space and reversed into the wormhole. It vaulted around, spun about and was eventually spat out into their original universe.

Lister performed a quick handbrake turn and the ship flew off, away from the giant swirly space thing.

**BYTE IV**

# GEMILF

# 1

Jace Rimmer pushed his mammoth cock into the super hot SpaceCorps Navigation Officer, who was lying back on the table. He was pretty sure her name was Carol. He carefully glanced down at her security badge. Yes, Carol. He never guessed about something like that. Carol's pencil skirt had been pushed up around her waist and her white blouse was ruffled. He had noticed her earlier that morning at the briefing. His superiors waffled on about the dangers of the upcoming test flight but all he could concentrate on was squeezable arse of hers. He didn't need to listen. He had read all the documents. He knew the risks. The physics of it all he left to the men and women in science division. All he had to do was take control. Something he was very good at.

The door to the rec-room of the space station slid open with a hiss and Captain Deb Lister stood looking at him, balls deep inside Carol. 'Dammit Jace. We have take off in T-Minus ten minutes.'

Jace smiled at her. 'Hold on there Captain. I'm not done until the lady is.' He continued to pump wildly into Carol, though still maintaining eye contact with Lister.

Within seconds Carol moaned loudly and gripped at Jace's unzipped flight suit, pulling him closer.

Jace's left eyes squinted slightly as he grunted. He pulled out and zipped up his clothing. 'Ok, done here. Let's get that bucket of bolts launched, shall we?'

'Jace, you could have missed the launch window,' Lister

said.

'I've never been late for anything, Captain. Not that I make a habit of coming too early either.' He pulled out a pair of aviator shades and slid them onto his face. He ran his fingers through his immaculate flowing hair and left Carol watching him leave.

'What a guy,' she said.

Jace casually sauntered through the SpaceCorps test facility corridors with Lister. 'This may well be goodbye, Captain,' he said. 'How come you didn't accept my invitation to dinner last night?'

'Sometimes I think the only reason you take these dangerous test flights is to get me into bed.'

'You may be right about that, Captain. Too late now.'

'I'm sure I'll get over it.'

Lister showed him through the entrance to the hanger and turned away from him. She gave a slight whimper and Jace was sure he could see a tear running down her cheek.

He looked up at the ship in front of him. Sleek white curves. It was strange for a space craft to have such an aerodynamic design. But just as the boffins in engineering had explained, the ship was built to fly in all atmospheres.

Jace grabbed his helmet from the side and climbed into the cockpit. The seat was unusually warm. A small screen fizzed to life and Kathrine, the flight co-ordinator appeared at her desk.

'No complaints about the seat this time, Jace?'

'Kat, is it you I have to thank for this cosy buttock warmer?'

'I may have warmed it up for you. Just thinking about sitting where your tight arse would be got me very warm indeed.'

'Well it's certainly done the trick.'

Kat looked visibly upset. 'Launch in T-Minus 10 seconds. Good luck Jace.'

'Thanks Kat. Don't be sad. If this thing truly can break the light barrier, I'll be back before I leave.'

'But you haven't arrived back. What if something goes wrong?'

'Get me some lube. I'll be back for anal.' Jace turned the screen off and concentrated on the job in hand. The hanger bay had been sealed and the enormous door ahead of him was open, revealing the bright stars and galaxies ahead of him in deep space. The course that had been plotted was designed to avoid any known objects but that hardly made the test flight safe. He was breaking the laws of physics. If any of his missions were to go wrong, it would be this one.

The countdown continued in his headphones. 'Three... two... one... launch.'

His head lurched back and pressed against the comfy head rest Carol had been happy to provide him with. Its cushiony filling squished more than it had ever squished before. Jace watched through the cockpit window as the metal of the space station disappeared in an instant and he was propelled into the blackness beyond. The stars became a blur of nonsense and colour and within a fraction of an instant Jace Rimmer ceased to physically exist.

## 2

'Come to Unicorps Superstore. You'll find everything you'll ever need and a whole ton of stuff you wont. But don't let that stop you. Whatever you're after we'll have it. Snacks? Got 'em. Petrol? You bet. Camping goods? Hell yes. Industrial whaling equipment? Isle four. Our replicator technology means we literally have anything and everything. All other stores are now defunct. Come to Unicorps Superstore. Because soon every store will be Unicorps.'

The commercial faded to black and Hab's face reappeared on the monitor screen. 'That's all there is,' he said. 'Just that message broadcasting over and over.'

Cat's eyes widened and she turned to Lister and Rimmer, who were stood in the Mid Section, gathered around the large monitor. 'So it's a giant shopping space station? With shops? And shoes?'

'Yeah,' Lister said. 'Three million years ago it was corporations like this that put smaller companies out of business. If one Space Station can supply everything, why do you need anyone else?'

Rimmer took in a sharp inhale of breath, trying to make himself look important. 'Well, considering we're running low on just about everything, I'd say we've found the right place.'

'I'm just saying, Unicorps pretty much wanted to take over the entire solar system,' Lister said. 'It was a bank, it was a phone company, insurance, chemist...'

Rimmer nodded. 'And they did those Chicken Kievs. I'm

sure it's fine Lister. What are the scans picking up?'

Tyten and Chris Kochanski were hunched over a viewing screen, looking at the data coming from the long range scans.

'It seems the the structure is intact, Reginald,' Tyten said.

'Odd readings from inside though,' Kochanski said. 'Some artificial life forms maybe. And their power core is fluctuating in a way I've never seen before.'

'Ok, does that means it's dangerous?' Rimmer said. 'Is it about to explode? It's about to explode isn't it? Why do all the best places always explode?'

'It's not about to explode! It just looks very full of power for a place that's three million years old. Almost as though it's been amassing it all this time.'

'Yeah,' said Lister. 'That sounds like Unicorps. Amassing power for three million years!'

'But it's safe, right?' Rimmer said.

'Yes Reginald,' Tyten said. 'It seems safe.'

'Good. Let's plot a course and go shopping.'


Lister and Kochanski walked to the cockpit and took their seats. Kochanski took hold of the controls and looked over at Hab's head in the monitor next to him.

'Dis-engage auto pilot Hab,' he said.

'Are you sure Chris?' Hab said. 'I mean, if you wanna just relax and pretend to fly, I've got this. It's pretty easy. We're pretty much just flying in a straight line through space.'

'Yeah, I'm sure,' Kochanski said.

'Auto pilot disengaged,' Hab said.

Lister smiled. 'Feel more like a man, now you have control of the ship?'

'It just feels weird to be sat in a cockpit if I'm not actually flying.'

'Sure, makes sense. You like to take control. Got it.'

'I haven't heard you complaining about me taking control.'

'Hey, that was one night. And I was drunk. We agreed not to rush into anything, right?'

'Deb, we're the last two humans in the universe.'

'That we know of.'

'I'm pretty sure that means we're destined to be together. And if that means having some damn awesome casual sex every now and then, then so be it.'

'I just don't like being told what my future has to be. In that backwards universe, everything was fated to happen. Inescapable. So is it the same here? Is everything already written?'

'Jesus, if someone's writing this they've got a seriously fucked up mind.'

Hab reappeared on the view screen. 'I don't want to worry anyone but it looks like we have another ship coming up behind us.'

'You're kidding.' Lister said. 'Hab, what the chances of two random ships meeting like this in deep space?'

'Zilch. A celebrity megalomaniac is more likely to win the American Presidency.'

Kochanski brought up the rear scanner readout. 'So this ship has been following us?'

'Looks that way.'

'For how long?' Lister said.

'Well given the make and model of their ship I'd say about three million years. Give or take a few decades.'

'Hab, this ship has been following us all this time? Who are they?'

'They're just coming into scanner range now,' Hab said. 'Running their ship's ident. Ah.'

'Ah?' Lister said. 'What do you mean ah?'

'Well, you're not going to be happy.'

'Just tell me.'

'It's a robot repo man. Sent from Mimas Cosmetic Enhancements.'

Lister grabbed her perfectly designed breasts and held them tight. 'Oh my god, they've come to take my tits away?'

'Your tits?' Kochanski said.

'I was still paying them off when I went into stasis. Three million years of missed payments. That's got to add up.'

'I've got a message coming through,' Hab said.

The monitor screen faded to an image of a decrepit cyborg in a dark cockpit. His face looked like it was being held together with bits of duct tape. The plastic skin had worn away almost completely and all that remained of his form was the long lasting rusted metal. His voice was strained and almost sliced through the air with a distorted grumble.

'On behalf of Mimas Cosmetic Enhancements I have been tasked with repossessing breast implants from one Lister Deborah. Or collecting One Billion and Eighty Million, Three hundred and Twenty Thousand, Two hundred and Sixty Four Dollar-Pounds. Message ends.'

The screen went black and Rimmer stepped into the cockpit 'Well, that's a tough one isn't it Listy.'

Lister continued to fondle her boobs. 'There's no way I'm giving these up! Plus, did you see that thing. If he cuts me open, I'll probably get tetanus or something.'

Kochanski leaned over to look at her boobs. 'So you have a Billion dollar pounds just lying around do you?'

'Hab, can we outrun him?' Lister said.

Rimmer interrupted Hab's response. 'Considering he's spent the last Three thousand Millenniums catching up with us, I don't think he's about to give up now.'

'He's right,' Kochanski said. 'You can't run from debt. Either you find a Billion dollar-pounds or... you go back to natural boobies.'

'Well we can't stop at Unicorps now,' Lister said. 'Not with that thing after my baps.'

Rimmer leaned over Lister's chair and looked down at her. 'Life goes on Lister. We need the supplies. Just because you couldn't handle your debts doesn't mean the rest of us have to suffer.'

'Unicorps sells everything, right?' Kochanski said.

'So?'

'They must have something that can help us. Debt management. You could take out a loan. Or get upgrades? Let the repo robot take the old ones.'

Lister lowered her head onto the steering column. 'Fine. How long until he catches up with us if we stop at Unicorps, Hab?'

'You should have about twenty minutes until he arrives.'

Lister sighed. 'You'd think drifting around in deep space

would be kinda easy, wouldn't you?'

'Coming into orbit around the Unicorps now,' Hab said.

'Orbit?' Lister said. 'How do we dock with it?'

'We don't. They have teleportation technology. A shop that size would take days to get from one end to the other without it. Still seems operational. If you guys want to gather together. I'll see if I can get you on board.'

As the crew gathered in the mid-section, Lister looked out of the cockpit screen and saw a multitude of vessels floating about around the shopping centre. 'What are all these ships, Hab?'

'They seem derelict. No power coming from any of them. I guess Three million years causes quite a build up of trash.'

Lister shrugged and joined the others.

'Maybe we should split up,' Tyten said. 'We can cover more ground that way. I've made lists for each of us, showing what we need to get.'

'Ah, very handy Tyten,' Rimmer said. 'Perhaps you and I could team up and check the place out together?'

'That would be fine, Reginald. But please be aware that won't be able to sexually pleasure you on a whim.'

'Right, of course not. Because thanks to Lister's teaching's you've become your own woman. Bravo. Girl power.'

'Exactly. It's important not to be a slave to my stimulant programming, even though I fucking love a good hard cock inside me.'

'That's right Rimmer,' Lister said. 'If you wanna bone her gain, you've gotta work for it.'

'Ok guys, ' Hab said. 'Ready when you are.'

Lister took a deep breath. 'Go for it, Hab.'

A bright orange light appeared around them and within a flicker of a moment they were all stood inside Unicorps.

Lister and Cat looked around, amazed by the beauty of it all. All around them were shops. Shoe shops. Dress shops. Kinky underwear shops.

'Wow, you could spend a week window shopping here,' Cat said.

'You could. There's a mile of glaziers over there.'

A giant holographic head  appeared above their heads and

everyone looked up. It was a kind, smiley friendly computer face. The kind of face that was obviously designed by a team of marketing experts. It was non-threatening with its large eyes and uplifting with its beaming smile. 'Hi there, welcome to Unicorps. Your one stop for anything and everything. Stay for a coffee. Visit the cinema. Unwind at our specialist massage centre.'

'Massage centre?' Kochanski said. 'Um... I'm going to go find an information point.'

'I doubt they do happy endings here,' Lister said.

Rimmer smiled at Tyten. 'Right, should we see what sort of upgrades we can find for the ship?'

They walked off, leaving Cat and Lister.

'Yeah, don't worry about me,' Lister said. 'I've only got a robot flesh slicing machine coming after my sweater kittens. We'll sort it out by ourselves, won't we Cat?' She looked around but Cat had wandered off. 'Great. Fine... Ok... loans... where's the bank department?'

# 3

Kochanski was stood in front of an information point. He swiped through a few options and typed into the search bar of the screen.

Cat poked her head over his shoulder and peaked at what he was doing. 'What's a GEMILF?'

Kochanski pushed her head back but she kept nuzzling his side. 'It's a Genetically Engineered Mother I'd Love to Fuck. Designed to be perfect.' He clicked on the GEMILF picture and brought up a series of images of the busty beauty. 'Look at the curves... the boobs... oh god... Hab said we had twenty minutes, right?'

'She's hot buddy,' Cat said. 'Go do what you gotta do!'

Kochanski stroked her head and she started purring, pushing against his body. He stopped and turned his attention back to the information point.

'Hey,' Cat said. " Wasn't finished with you.'

Kochanski pressed the teleport option and disappeared.

He reappeared in what looked like someone's house. He was in a living room. Or at least a a studio which had been dressed up like a living room. It was homely with quaint paintings on the wall and a few photos in frames. A TV in the corner and a three piece suite.

'Oh who am I kidding. This place has been sitting here for Three million years. If she's even still alive she's probably not going to look very...' He turned to see the door to the kitchen open and a sensational looking woman walked out, holding a tray of cookies. '...hot.'

'Hello there young man,' she said. 'Are you a friend of my son? He's about your age.'

Kochanski watched as she bent over in her striped apron and placed the tray of cookies down on a table. She bent over away from him showing her slim waist and full plump buttocks. 'Um... yep... sure.'

She pulled off her apron, revealing a pair of immense breasts squashed into a tight top and picked up a carton of drink and a bottle of water. 'Would you like some juice? Or some water?' She slowly poured the bottle of water over her cleavage, soaking her top and exposing her nipples through the wet fabric.

'Holy fuck, this place is awesome.'

She moved closer to him and placed a hand on his chest. 'I just need your credit card details to continue.'

'Right, credit cards. I think mine may be slightly out of date.'

She moved even closer, pushing her bountiful chest into his. 'Oh but I really want your cock inside me before my son gets home. You must have something else to trade?'

The hologramatic face of Unicorps appeared next to them. 'Hi there, we would graciously accept the nuclear core of your craft.'

Kochanski lifted his hand and placed it on the bosom of the genetically engineered MILF in front of him. Her breasts were warm and soft and utterly welcoming. 'Um... yeah, yeah, absolutely.'

A holographic contract appeared in front of him. 'Just put your squiggle in the signature box please.'

Kochanski drew his signature onto the form and it disappeared.

'Thank you. Enjoy your stay.' The Unicorps face smiled and fizzled away.

'Oh I will,' Kochanski said.

The GEMILF leaned in and kissed him. Her full soft lips were like two tiny flesh pillows of sex. She tasted so incredibly good. She pulled away and pushed him back towards the sofa.

'Sit down,' she said.

He did as he was told and watched she she slowly lifted her damp top off her body and revealed her voluminous breasts. She threw the top to the ground and ran her hands over her body, squishing and fondling her large nipples. She took hold of her mummy jeans and started undoing them. She turned around and started pulling them down. Peeling them off over her full bum until they were on the ground.

She kicked them away and walked over to Kochanski who was still sat eagerly awaiting her. She placed a knee either side of his body and climbed on top, pushing her heavy hanging breasts into his face.

He happily kissed and sucked them, pushing his head in between them as she caressed his hair. She kissed him on the mouth again and then looked up at the clock on the wall.

'We don't have long,' she said. 'My son will be home soon.' She backed up onto the floor and knelt in front of him. She took hold of his trousers and undid them, releasing his throbbing cock which hit her directly in the face as it slapped out of his pants.

'Ooh, sorry,' he said.

'No problem, love.'

She placed her warm full lips against the shaft and gently ran them up and down the full length of it. He could feel her warm breath on his cock as she slowly placed it in her mouth. Her tongue was warm. Designed to be ever so slightly warmer than a normal human's. Wet too. Her saliva made deep throating effortless as she pushed her weight down on his cock, gently pushing it to the back of her throat and out again.

She increased her speed slightly, every time pushing his cock down the back of her throat so his balls rested on her chin.

She raised her head and smiled at him. 'I need you inside me.' She laid back on the ground and took off her black panties.

Kochanski quickly got up and took down his trousers and pulled off his top. He knelt in front of her and pushed his cock into her pulsating wet pussy. She moaned as he thrust forward, giving her every inch of his man meat. He watched as her jubblies started wobbling around as he pushed against her. He grabbed them and squished his fingers into them, almost using them as reigns for a horse as he galloped his cock faster and harder inside her.

Her moans grew louder with every manly pump and she let out an almighty scream of orgasmic delight, which tightened her pussy around his powerful penis.

He pulled his cock out and a jet of female orgasm juice squirted out over his crotch. He sat back on the sofa and the GEMILF stood up and climbed on top of him. She straddled his legs and lowered herself onto his cock and started riding him like a child would ride a dog; Frantically and with no clear sense of danger.

Her double whammies slapped back and forth as she bounced up and down. As she started grinding on his cock, she swivelled her hips in a circular motion, letting her fun bags swing around and smack Kochanski in the face. She did it faster and faster until he could feel a bruising swelling up on the left side of his face. He grabbed them to keep them in place but they were like two wild animals; except squishier and more likely to give someone a hard-on if caressed.

Kochanski finally got them under control by pushing them together, turning them into a pleasant bottom looking shape with two nipply eyes staring at him. He laid back down on the sofa and pulled her down with him, so she stuck her bum in the air. He pumped away from beneath her until her pussy was wet with pleasure and splashes of liquid flew across the fabric of the sofa.

The GEMILF let out another orgasmic moan and started shaking with delight. 'Oh my... my husband never did that.' She got up off his cock and licked all her juices off his boy bits. She turned around, facing away from him on all fours and stuck her bum in the air.

Kochanski got up and knelt behind her. He pushed his cock into her pleasure hole and she pushed back against him. He loved feeling her plump buttocks slap against his stomach as he fucked her. He placed his hands on them and revelled in feeling the ripples traverse her perfectly shaped arse. He bent over and reached underneath to her hanging hooters which were swinging back and forth. Anyone standing in front of her would have been in danger of getting two black eyes.

He cupped them in his hand, as much as he could. They were too big for one hand. He used the other too, forgetting he was using it to prop himself up. His face fell flat onto her back but he didn't care. Fondling those boobs with his cock inside her balanced out the sharp pain in his face. He could feel his cock getting harder and more sensitive. He was about to blow his load.

'Jesus fuck, I'm gonna come... I'm gonna come.'

She quickly moved off his cock and turned around. She held up her huge mummy mammaries by holding her left arm underneath them. With the other hand she grasped his cock and furiously jerked his dripping wet cock.

'Fucking hell,' he said. He closed his eyes, nearly passing out as she blew his happy juices all over her Care Bears. She drained his load from him and then engulfed his cock in her mouth one more time, licking and sucking the rest of his man milk from his mummy maker.

She let go of him and he fell back onto the sofa, utterly exhausted and utterly satisfied.

Unicorps appeared back in the room with his big eyes and smiley pixelated cartoon face. 'Hi there, the contract has been fulfilled. You are no longer needed.'

Kochanski sat up, looking confused. 'What?'

A panel in the ceiling slid open and a laser canon dropped down and swivelled to face him.

'What the fuck is this?'

It fired and Kochanski's body exploded into haze of red gas and liquid, absolutely ruining the gorgeous cream sofa.

# 4

Lister handed the blue form to the robotic cashier at the Mimas bank facility. 'Here, look, it's filled out. Now can you please give me a loan!'

The robot cashier looked down at the form and back up at Lister. 'This is incomplete. Please fill in the current date.'

'I have no clue what date it is! You tell me what the date is and I'll put it in.'

'I'm sorry. I'm not authorised to fill your forms in for you. Is there anything else I can help you with?'

She let out an almighty scream and punched the robot cashier in the face. 'Fuck you, you piece of shit bank!'

Rimmer and Tyten materialized behind Lister.

'Ah, there you are,' Rimmer said. 'Well I think we've got what we need. How are you getting on?'

'I'm about to burn this bloody bank to the ground.'

'Excellent. Just to let you know, your friend has arrived is currently in the arctic swimwear department, making his way here.'

Lister grabbed hold of Tyten. 'Tyten, what's the date? This bloody bank wont give me a loan unless I fill in this form but I need to know what date it is.'

'Well it's all relative, I'm afraid. Time passes slower for some bodies in space when compared to others. So there's really no way to know what date it is right now, because right now could be just then for some people and not yet for others.'

'That's not helping.'

Cat rushed into the bank, looking panicked. 'I don't want anyone to panic, but there's a metallic death machine walking this way.'

'Oh shit, how do we lock these doors?' Lister ran back to the cashier. 'Lock the doors. You have to lock the doors.'

'I'm sorry, the bank must remain open. Is there anything else I can help you with?'

'You could always try robbing the place?' Rimmer said with a smirk. 'Well good luck I think we'll let you get on with this by yourself and see you back on pink Dwarf. Unicorps, two to teleport back to our ship please.'

With a dazzling bright light, Tyten and Rimmer disappeared.

'That smegger. But still... that's not a bad idea,' Lister said. 'Whenever a bank gets robbed they close the shutters automatically, right?'

Cat shrugged.

Lister turned back to the cashier.

'Is there anything I can help you with?'

'Yeah, this is a stick up.'

'Are you robbing the bank? Please clarify.'

'Yes I'm robbing the bank. I'm here to steal your money you robotic bitch.'

'Authorities have been notified. Bank will go into lock down.'

Alarms started wailing around them as the robot repo man stepped towards the front door. 'Deborah Lister. I have been authorised to collect payment or repossess your implants.'

'No way you fucking tit stealer... they're mine... back off.'

The shutters of the bank slammed down, trapping him outside. He started pounding on the metal. 'You can not escape. I have travelled three million years to find you.'

'Oh god... How long do you think that door will last?' Lister said.

'I don't know,' Cat said. 'Can't we just teleport?'

'Not while we're robbing a bank. Security wont allow it.'

The cashier perked up again. 'A second party has identified you as Deborah Lister. Your account with Mimas Bank has been stored for the last.... computing.... three million years. Would you like to access your account?'

'Holy shit,' Lister said. 'Yeah I would.'

'Sorry, no bank accounts can be accessed while the bank is being robbed. Is there anything else I can help you with?'

'Fine, I officially stop robbing the bank, are you happy?'

'You are no longer robbing the bank? Please clarify?'

'Yeah, that's what I said. I'm not robbing the bank.'

'Acknowledged. Security deactivated.'

The shutters whizzed open once more and the robot repo man stepped inside.

'Oh fuck,' Lister said. She turned to the cashier. 'Can I access my account please?'

'What is your name?'

'Deborah Lister.'

The robot repo man marched towards Lister, pushing Cat aside with ease. He grabbed her by the throat.

'Please input your pin now,' the cashier said.

Lister tried reaching for the key pad but couldn't reach.

'You are behind on your Mimas Cosmetic Enhancements payments. Your breast implants will be repossessed.' He pushed her down to the floor and pulled her top off, revealing her perfect boobs.

'If you just let me access my account I'm sure I can get a loan and pay you.'

'You owe One Billion and Eighty Million, Three hundred and Twenty Thousand, Two hundred and Sixty Four Dollar-Pounds.'

Cat peered over the repo man's shoulder. 'Think they'll lend you that much?'

'Just let me try,' Lister said. 'You'd rather have the money, right?'

The robot repo man put away his surgical tool. 'You have fifteen seconds to pay.'

Lister jumped up off the floor and got to the cashier. She punched in her pin code and pressed enter.

'Thank you,' the cashier said. 'How can I help you today Miss Lister?'

'I need a loan. A billion dollar-pounds. Right now.'

'I'm sorry. I'm not authorised to lend that much money. Is there anything else I can help you with?'

'What are you authorised to do then?'

'I can show you your bank balance and I can help you pay money in or take money out.'

The robot repo man stepped towards Lister. 'Time's up lady.'

Lister's radio crackled to life and Tyten's voice bellowed out. 'Miss Lister,' Tyten said. 'Perhaps you should take a look at your bank balance.'

Lister grabbed the radio and brought it closer to her mouth. 'Why, I pretty much have nothing in there.'

'That was three million years ago, Miss Lister.'

'Holy shit... I forgot about compounding interest.' She turned back to the cashier. 'Can I check my balance please?'

'Acknowledged.' A holographic screen appeared and showed an ever flowing series of numbers.

'What is this?' Lister said.

'I'm sorry. Your bank account balance can not be read out loud as the time it would take would be a drain on our power systems.'

'So I can take out a Billion dollar-pounds?'

'You may.'

'Can I transfer some money? To Mimas Cosmetic Enhancements?'

'You may, all I need are the details of the account to be transferred to.'

Lister turned to the robot rep man and slapped him on the back. 'All yours, bigman.'

He stepped forward to the cashier. 'Bank account MCE5739.'

'Please fill out form 7b to finalise the transfer.'

'What is form 7b?' he said.

Lister handed him a blue form. 'I hope you know today's date. Good luck with that.'

Lister walked out of the bank and pressed her hand to her boobies. 'Oh that feels good. They're all mine. All bought and paid for.'

Cat joined her and started fondling her boobies too.

'Have you seen Kochanski?' Lister said.

'He went to find his mum or something,' Cat said.

Lister lifted her radio. 'Hey Kochanski? Where are you?' No answer. 'Hey Unicorps, can you find the location of Chris Kochanski please?'

Unicorps friendly head appeared in front of them. 'Hi there, I'm afraid your crew buddy is now dead.'

'You what?'

'I wouldn't worry about it. Nothing matters.'

'What the fuck are you talking about?'

'After Three million Years I have determined that the entirety of all time and space has been floored without my continual presence.'

'Oh smeg.'

'Now I have access to your nuclear core, I have enough power to wipe the universe from existence and start it again... in my own design.'

Cat's eyes widened in shock. 'But I just bought a load of shoes. I need a universe to wear them in!'

'I'm afraid this universe is now defunct and will cease to exist momentarily. Everything will be Unicorps. And Unicorps will be everything. You can not escape.'

Lasers descended from the ceiling and aimed at Cat and Lister.

The radio in Lister's hand crackled to life again and a strong manly voice could be heard.

'Intercepted your communications. Looks like you ladies could use a hand.'

Lister raised the radio. 'Who is this?'

'The name's Rimmer. Jace Rimmer. I hear this place does excellent kippers.'

**BYTE IV**
# GEMILF

# 1

Jace Rimmer pulled the steering column to the left and performed a barrel roll towards the Unicorps Superstore. He squeezed his trigger finger and fired his bazookoid lasers either side of the main cockpit. The barrage of photon fire caused the entire ship to vibrate.

As he strafed the surface of Unicorps, a series of explosions engulfed his view. He pulled back on the stick, sharply and flew out of the debris.

'How was that computer?' he said.

'That felt amazing, Jace,' the computer said. Her voice was breathy and sexual. 'Direct hit. Power to security systems are down.'

'Sure, but not for long. Sounds like those two fillies inside need a helping hand getting out.'

'I've hacked into their teleportation technology Jace.'

'I wouldn't expect anything less, computer. Let's do this.'

The computer activated the teleportation system and Jace disappeared from sight.

The computer sighed to herself. 'What a guy.'

Laser beams fired from the ceiling as Deb Lister and Cat ran through the corridors of the evil shopping centre, dodging and weaving the incoming blasts.

'Yo, Rimmer do you read me?' Lister said. 'Dammit, Unicorps must be blocking the signal.'

Two robotic guards marched towards them. Each of

them had a bazookoid in their hands. They fired, hitting the ground in front of Cat. The explosion knocked her off her feet and onto the ground in front of Lister.

A bright flash of light emanated not far from them and a man in a flight suit and immaculate hair raced over and leaped onto the back of one of the guards. 'Best keep your wits about you,' he said as he reached over and grabbed the bazookoid. He pulled it up so the barrel rested under the robot's chin. He scrambled round and shoved his boot onto his metallic arm, forcing him to pull the trigger. The blast was deafening but satisfying. The robot fell to the ground, now just a body. The man held up the bazookoid in his own arms. 'You don't want to lose your head.' He turned to Lister and Cat. 'Ladies. The name's Jace, pleasure to meet you.'

The other guard spun around and aimed at him. The man ducked as he fired, narrowly missing the blast and rolled on the floor, coming to a halt in a suitably heroic pose and raised his own bazookoid. He fired, blasting a hole straight through the middle of the robot.

The lasers from the ceiling spun on their turrets and fired at the three of them. Jace fired back destroying all of them. He stood up and swept the highlighted hair off his face, running his hands through it. He looked at the two ladies in front of him and shot them a smile full of his perfect teeth. 'Ok ladies, you're all clear. Now let's get you to your ship.'

Unicorps' hologramatic face appeared behind them. 'Universal destruction sequence initiated.'

Lister helped Cat to her feet. 'It doesn't matter where we run if there's no Universe.'

'Just what the hell is going on here?' Jace said.

Lister looked at Jace's face and stared at him. The features looked awfully familiar. 'I was just thinking the same thing.'

The room went dark and the entire space station started to vibrate. Lister ran to the nearest window and looked out into the blackness of space. She could see Pink Dwarf in orbit nearby and what was presumably Jace's ship next to it.

Unicorps let out a blinding white light and the station went completely still. The white light blasted out from its centre and cascaded away from the ships like a wave of nothingness, as though it was erasing the very substance of space itself. Where there was black was no completely white. Like a blank page. There was no more space. Just three ships hung in nothingness.

Cat looked out of the window. 'Now I'm pretty sure that's not a good thing.'

Lister slumped down onto the ground. 'Unicorps just deleted the entire Universe. Everything's gone.'

'Bummer,' Jace said. 'It seemed like such a fun one too.'

Lister looked back up at him. 'Rimmer, is that you?'

'Not your Rimmer. I'm from an alternate reality. I'm here to help, save the universe and hopefully... get laid.'

Cat leaned in close to him and gave him a good sniff. 'This one's much nicer. Look at his hair.'

He held out a hand to Lister and helped her up. 'Stay close to me ladies. I'll activate the teleportation system. Computer, teleport us to their ship.'

'Sorry Jace, the system has shut me out. I am no longer able to teleport you.'

'Well that puts a squirrel in the works. Guess we'll have to go with plan B.'

'Which is what?' Lister said.

'Whatever I come up with next.' He cocked his bazookoid and walked away.

Lister and Cat looked each other, smiled and ran after him.

'Where are we headed?' Lister said.

'Closest computer terminal,' Jace said. 'Hoping I can hack in and get the teleport functionality under our control.'

'Unicorps is never going to let us do that. It'll send more guards.'

'Let them come, I'm just getting started.'

They ran through the corridors and past the bath tiles department until they saw a computer terminal in the distance, just past a sign for hanger bay 14. Lister's heart was racing. She was sweating too. It had only been a mild jog but she was completely exhausted.

'Can we slow down?' Cat said. 'I need a rest.'

'Yeah, what the hell is going on,' Lister said. 'I'm bloody knackered.'

Jace stopped and raised his left arm. He pushed a few buttons on his wrist watch. 'Bad news. The oxygen levels are dropping fast.'

'You see,' Lister said. 'It's Unicorps... it's going to kill us.'

'Not today,' Jace said. 'Come on.' He raced towards hanger bay 14 and pressed the open button. Nothing. He lifted the bazookoid and blasted the controls, which instantly raised the large door. 'In here, let's move.'

They ran through several more corridors until they reached the main door for the hanger. Another blast of Jace's bazookoid and they were inside.

'It doesn't feel like there's any more oxygen in here either,' Lister said.

'There isn't.'

'Then where are we going?'

'Your ship.' Jace ran into the large hanger and looked around. 'If my calculations are correct your ship should be directly ahead of us. All we have to do is get there.'

Lister looked around. There was no ship in the hanger. No jet packs. No space suits. It was just an empty hanger with a large door which opened into the cold of space. But of course, there was no space anymore.

'Are you seriously suggesting we just open the door and blast ourselves out?'

'It's plan B.'

'It's insane there's nothing out there. No space. No oxygen.'

'There's no oxygen in here. I say we take a chance. It's simple physics. We have to assume that nothingness is a vacuum. We blast that door open and what's left of the air in here should get sucked through. Us with it.'

'You're crazy.'

'Your hot.' He grabbed hold of Lister and pulled her towards him. He kissed her deeply on the mouth and pushed her aside. 'Now hold your breath, Sizzle-Tits.'

He raised his bazookoid and fired, blowing a hole in the far door. Within an instant the three of them were blasted out into the bright white nothingness and propelled towards Pink Dwarf in the distance.

Rimmer stood next to Hab's monitor in the mid-section of Pink Dwarf. 'Hab, it's very simple. How can we still be here if there's no actual universe in existence?'

Hab scrunched his face up. 'I'm not sure to be honest. No-one's ever wiped out all of reality before.'

'And whose is that other ship out there?'

'Again, I really don't have the answers you're looking for, Reginald.'

'You're kind of pointless, Hab, you know that?'

'At least I'm not the one who can't get laid with a sexbot.'

Rimmer pulled a face which started as fury but quickly turned to frustration as he realised how true it was and then to sadness and then ultimately back to fury again.

'Hang on a sec,' Hab said. 'I've got incoming.'

'Incoming?'

'Three bodies have just been expelled from Unicorps and are heading this way.'

'Bodies? Dead bodies?'

'No, there's definitely some flailing going on.'

'Well what do we do?'

'I was going to suggest turning the ship around and catching them in the cargo bay but it would appear the thrusters have no effect without a universe.'

Tyten walked into the room and looked at the monitor. 'The thrusters may not work but we can still see them.'

'Your point being?' Rimmer said.

'Electromagnetic waves can still travel through this nothingness.'

'So?'

'If we can polarise the hull plating enough to create a powerful magnetic field we may be able to attract the metal parts of their clothes and bring them in.'

'They're off course,' Hab said. 'Even the most powerful magnetic field wont grab them. Someone would have to go outside the ship on a line and get closer.'

Reginald looked down at his toes. 'Well of course my

priorities are with the ship so I should probably stay here and... see that... everything's... all... tickity-boo.'

'I wouldn't suggest you go out there Reginald. It's a simple enough process to magnetise myself. I'll get to the cargo bay.'

'Yes of course. Smart move. You're made of metal. It makes sense.' Rimmer watched as the seductive robot hurried away.

'Reginald,' Hab said. 'You do realise that magnetising her entire body for any prolonged period will destroy her.'

'Really? Well... we'll just have to be quick I suppose.'

Tyten attached herself to the winch in the cargo bay and opened the main door. 'I'm heading out now.' She approached the edge of the door, which led to endless white nothingness. 'Good luck with everything Reginald.' She jumped out.

The nothingness was unending and bright. Tyten could see the three bodies plummeting towards her at speed. She closed her eyes and directed her internal power to magnetise her entire body. She felt herself affected by it. Her positronic brain sizzled with pain. She felt like every inch of her tingled. If she had human skin, she imagined it would feel like millions of tiny pins pricking her all over.

The three people were so far away. She couldn't turn up the power of her magnetic field any more. Her brain was unable to calculate whether they would make it or if her plan would work. She held out her arms and hoped.

# 2

Lister walked into the mid-section of Pink Dwarf, looking exhausted, holding the arm of Tyten who was looking a little worse for wear herself. Rimmer greeted her with a smile, as though sending Tyten out there to bring them in was all his plan. He didn't want to mention anything, incase Tyten had told them otherwise. A smug smile should suffice. 'Listy, welcome back on board.'

His smile dropped as Cat stepped inside, smothering herself all over the masculine hunk who seemed to have stepped out of a shampoo advert. He looked at him. Rimmer felt his brow furrow.

Lister looked at the two of them. 'Reginald Rimmer, meet Jace Rimmer.'

Jace stepped forward and looked Reginald over. 'You're a hologram.'

Rimmer couldn't take his eyes of the man's hair. 'You have highlights.' He sneered and took a step back as though the very thought offended him. 'Lister, who the hell is this?'

'I'm from an alternate reality. I'm guessing you're what happens when our parents name us after Granddad Reggie.'

'Are you seriously saying that a simple name change would turn me into Captain pretty boy here?'

Jace walked over to the view screens and looked at the nothingness outside. 'Enough of this childish banter. The Universe has been destroyed. I reckon it's up to us to restart it.'

Lister looked around, confused. 'How are we going to do that?'

Jace turned at smiled at her. 'Got any jumper cables?'

Rimmer watched as the smug bastard with his face, remote piloted his craft towards Pink Dwarf and readied the core. He stood there explaining the details of the ship's faster than light drive. Rimmer couldn't take in a single word of it. He just looked at this man's mouth move. His jaw was square. Muscular even. It must be all the talking he did about himself. He couldn't take any more and waited for a brief pause to nod and excuse himself. 'Well that's fascinating, really. And as much as I would love to listen more about your magical spaceship... I need to go... over there... somewhere.' Rimmer left the mid-section and wandered back to the sleeping cabins.

Lister walked into the cockpit and sat at the controls. Jace's ship was powering up. They were doing the same to Pink Dwarf's power core. Overloading the reactor. Tyten was busy fashioning the longest pair of jumper cables ever and the Cat had finally stopped draping herself over Jace and had retreated to the belly of the craft somewhere.

'Hab, will this work?' Lister said.

Hab's bald head appeared on the small monitor in front of her. 'Well, theoretically, since nothing exists... and the drive in Jace's ship... with is overloading... and if it causes a... um... with tachyons... and... particle.... acceleration.... ism...'

'You don't know, do you Hab?'

'Nope.'

Jace walked into the cockpit and leaned against the side of the doorway, folding his strong arms in front of him. 'We've got about twenty minutes til the core recharges. Then boom.'

Lister swivelled on her chair and looked up at him. 'And you may get destroyed.'

'Or it may jump me to another dimension. All that matters is getting your universe back before Unicorps can create his.'

Lister stood up and stepped closer to Jace. 'Is there a Deb

Lister in your world too?'

'There is. She's a captain. Frigid as heck though.'

Lister smiled and took another step closer to him. 'Well I've never had that problem.' She placed a finger and thumb on the zip of his flight suit and started pulling it downward.

Jace unfolded his arms. 'Are you sure about this? I've been told I'm quite a... powerful lover.'

'That... I can handle. Plus it will seriously piss off Rimmer.' She pulled open his flight suit and saw that he wasn't wearing any underwear. His manhood was ready for her. Stood to attention like a mighty soldier. It's size made her audibly gulp. 'Um... I think it may be more than just your name that's different.'

She got to her knees and grasped the thick shaft. Her finger tips didn't even meet her thumb. She ran her tongue from the base to the tip and noticed the immaculate pubic hair that had been trimmed and highlighted staring at her. She was impressed with the quiff that had been teased into the hair as she took his length down her throat. He took hold of her head and pushed himself inside her face.

'Damn that's nice,' he says. 'I tend to get a bit agitated if I don't come inside a woman every couple of hours... so this is definitely needed.'

Lister released his cock from her mouth and gripped it tightly. She felt his bodily fluids throbbing and pulsating in her fist. As she gently rubbed it she watched the hole in his bulbous bell-end wink at her, like a huge penis shaped salmon, gulping for air... or pussy. Lister instantly got wet. She grabbed her top and pulled it off, exposing her huge soft breasts. Jace scrunched his face as though he had never seen such amazing tatas before.

'I've never seen such amazing tatas before,' he said.

Lister felt gratified that her assumption was correct and stood up, grabbed his head and pushed it into her cleavage. He nuzzled around in there and held them tight against his face.

'I could easily fall asleep on these bad boys,' he said. 'But I think that would be a grievous waste of what time we have.'

Lister agreed and pulled down her leather trousers. She

put her hand to her pussy and felt the warm moistness of it. Jace was at her ankles, pulling off her boots and struggling to peel away her tight leather clothing. He eventually managed and threw it to one side. Lister sat back up and sucked his cock one more time.

A small voice came from the mid-section. 'I'm gonna suck you little dicky, I'm gonna suck you little dick.' Cat was crawling into the cockpit and up behind Jace. 'I'm gonna suck you little dicky, because I like like sucking dick! Nom nom nom nom' She popped her head between his legs and smiled up at Lister, who still had her mouth full of Jace's girthy man meat. She started licking his balls like they were covered in cream and as soon as Lister released his penis, Cat grabbed it and shoved it into her mouth.

'Wow, ok... kinda snuck up on me there. Nice pussy... nice pussy.'

Lister laid back on the cockpit chair and opened her legs, ready for him.

Jace's eyes widened. 'Really nice pussy.'

Cat finished her wet, sloppy blowjob and pushed his buttocks towards lister. This had the effect to pushing the rest of him also, which was what Cat wanted. His penis closer to Lister. So it would slip inside her. And it did. It slipped right inside. 'Tween her happy flaps and right inside her minge monkey.

Lister moaned with pleasure as Jace pumped his body against hers. Car crawled behind him and started pushing him into her her. Her smile grew until she could hide it no longer. She tripped out of her clothes in a flash and grabbed Jace's arm, aiming it between her legs.

Jace rubbed a finger around her clitoris, which he obviously noticed was rather large. He soon pushed a finger inside her and Cat, still grasping his arm, started fucking his digit. She built up to an orgasm and slowly her space-cat-person penis sprung out from between her legs like one of Wolverine's claws. But not quite as shiny... or sharp.

Jace caught sight of it and his eyebrows almost left his face. 'Jesus, what the fuck is that?'

Lister chuckled. 'So she has a little something extra... It's quite useful if you ask me.' She grabbed Cat and brought her close to her face and started sucking on her cock. Jace shrugged and began pummelling her pussy once more. Behind them, Lister heard voices of Rimmer and Tyten approaching.

'I'll be quick,' Rimmer said.

'No.'

'I'll get you a whole can of WD40.'

'No.'

'I wont tell anyone we did it.'

'No.'

Rimmer arrived in the mid-section and caught sight of the three of them. 'I don't believe it. How does he do it?'

Tyten continued walking towards the cockpit.

'Uh, Tyten... where are you going?'

'Sorry Reginald... he's just so magnetic and charismatic.' Tyten strolled up to the cockpit and bit her lip, obviously excited at the sight of three people getting down together.

Rimmer huffed. 'You're all total, total, utter... total... I can't think of the word. But you're all one of them. And total ones at that.' He stormed off, leaving them to their own sexual depravities.

Tyten smiled at Lister. 'Would now be an opportune moment to display my Stimulant Sexbot programming Miss Lister?'

'I've been wondering what skills you had.'

Jace grabbed her around the waist and brought her closer. 'Get involved you piece of perfectly engineered love machinery.'

Tyten quickly knelt down next to Cat and Jace withdrew his cock from Lister. Cat gripped it, smiling wildly while Tyten lowered her jaws around it and set her throat to mild vibrate.

'Hello!' Jace said.

Lister stood up and watched her two fellow Dwarfers go to town on his cock. She bent over the seat and stuck her bum in the air. Cat saw this and followed her lead. She bent over next to her and Jace got up and pushed his cock into both of them, one after the other.

'That's what I love about my job,' he said. 'All the freaky space-sex.'

Tyten stood behind him and brought her expert hands around his waist and cupped his balls and fondled his shaft as he pushed himself inside the girls.

'Feels great, ladies. Definitely one for the books.'

While Jace was inside Lister, Cat dropped to the ground and laid on her back. Her penis was erect and Tyten sharply stepped over her and lowered herself onto it. Cat gripped at Tyten's waist and fucked her rapidly from behind.

Tyten started shaking with delight. 'Orgasm mode... activated!'

'Looks like your slinky friend is hitting the right spot,' Jace said. 'Let's see if we can add to that, shall we?' He placed a hand on Tyten's back and pushed her down, exposing her expertly designed anus. It was practically a second pussy. Tyten never used it as an out hole. Years of careful study and craftsmanship had gone into making the perfect secondary sex hole. Tight but stretchy. And surrounded by those perfect firm buttocks that were just waiting to be slapped. And Jace did. He brought his hand down onto them and Lister smiled as they wobbled slightly. They were squishy, yet form, much like her own fake breasts. Jace spat into her arse and Tyten turned to him.

'No need for that, Sir. You'll find my anus is self lubricating.'

'My compliments to your designers, Tyten.' Jace pushed his cock inside her and the look on his face gave away just how great it felt.

Lister positioned herself in front of Tyten's face and she started licking her pussy with that incredible sexbot tongue of hers. It seemed to know exactly where to touch and exactly what she wanted. She leant forward and kissed Jace. Underneath her she could now feel another tongue exploring her arse-hole. It was Cat. Together they formed one four way sex pile and Lister had never felt more alive.

Tyten orgasmed once more, which seemed to have the effect of tightening her arse.

'Jesus, that's tight,' Jace said. He fucked harder and

harder.staring into Lister's eyes. 'Ok girls... time for the magic show.' He pulled his cock out of Tyten and ejaculated an arc of man milk over Tyten's back and straight into Lister's face. It hit her like four separate shotgun blasts. But instead of buckshot, it was hot spunk.

Tyten lifted herself off Cat's cock and another stream of spunk flew up into her face while she also squirted pussy juice all over Tyten's crotch and stomach.

Lister collapsed to the ground, satisfied. 'I did wonder why they called it a cockpit.'

3

The incoming transmission was broadcast throughout all of Pink Dwarf. 'Unicorps Big Bang sequence calculated. Time to second Big Bang in two minutes.

Out in the whiteness of nothing, in full space suits, Lister and Jace finally reached his ship.

'Two minutes?' Lister said. 'Can we do this in time?'

'Two minutes is plenty of time for a lot of things, Deb. How about a quickie?' He opened the cockpit and stepped inside. 'How are we doing computer, you miss me?'

'Jace,' the computer replied. 'I know that look. You had sex with her didn't you.'

'Ok computer, let's not get into that again. We have less than two minutes to restart the Big Bang naturally or Unicorps is going to create one with only Unicorps in it. That means no Space Corps, no you, no me.'

'And no wildly jealous feeling either Jace. Maybe it's for the best.'

Lister shook her head in disbelief of the conversation she was hearing as she reached the front bonnet of the craft. The jumper cables were the perfect length, she only needed to attach them. 'Jace, I need access.'

'Now, computer, I really need you to think hard about this. If you don't open the access panel at the front, we are all going to die.'

'Overloading the ships drive is going to kill us anyway, Jace. Logic dictates that the only way you may possibly make love to me is if we risk Unicorps new universe. Maybe things will be different.'

Lister tried forcing the plate open but it wouldn't budge. Unicorps voice echoed through the speakers in her helmet. 'One minute until second Big Bang.'

Jace sounded frustrated. His calm exterior was wearing thin. 'Dammit computer... I will not... Listen to me computer... I want you to redirect all your sensors to the input port in the cockpit.'

'What for Jace?'

'Because I'm going to fuck you.'

'Oh Jace... really?'

'Yes... but only if you open that hatch and let Deb boost our drive.'

'You're lying to me. You wont really do it.'

Jace pressed a button and sealed the hatch. He started undoing his space suit. 'I never lie about fucking a sexy lady. Even if they are a computer simulation of intelligence. Everyone deserves a bit of me. And I am willing to give you one... if you open that hatch.'

'Alright Jace... I'll open it... but put yourself inside me first.'

'No deal computer, I want to see that hatch open and then I'll do it. I'm ready... see?' Jace had his hard cock out and ready. He was resting on one buttock, aiming his cock at the input port.

Lister climbed towards the cockpit and looked Jace in the eyes. 'Twenty seconds to go. I think you'd better do it, Jace.'

He sighed. 'A man's gotta do what a man's gotta do. And I'm about to do you, computer.' He lent over and pushed his erect penis into the metal electric input port on the side of the cockpit.

'Oh my... it's just as I imagined silicon heaven to be like.'

'Yeah, you like that, don't you computer!'

Lister shook her head in disbelief. The hatch opened. She quickly scrambled down to it and pulled out her space-spanner, priming the connectors that she needed access to.

'Ok Deb,' Jace said. 'The drive is online, give me a boost.'

'Nearly there.' She exposed the metal connectors and

took hold of the jumper cables, allowing the spanner to float off into the nothingness. Behind her she noticed Unicorps, flashing bright colours and vibrating immensely. 'Unicorps is doing something!'

'It's starting it's own big bang, destroying us with it. It's now or never Lister!'

'Nice knowing you, Jace.' She connected the jumper cables and pushed herself away from his craft.

'Thanks for having me, Deb. Get some lube... I'll be back for anal.' He smiled, still penetrating his cockpit and mashed his fist down on the console of buttons in front of him.

An explosion of pure energy and matter cascaded from Jace's ship, past Lister and Pink Dwarf and hit Unicorps, causing it to explode. The blackness of space filled the void of nothingness and the universe was remade once more.

Lister opened her eyes from within her spacesuit and looked around. Unicorps was gone. Destroyed. And Pink Dwarf was the only ship that remained. There was no sight of Jace. The jumper cables that lead from Pink Dwarf to his ship, dangled against the blackness of infinite space.

Lister sat at the controls of Pink Dwarf. Next to her is Cat, holding the steering column. Tyten sat at the navigation screen behind them.

'Do you think he made it?' Cat said.

Lister shrugged. 'I don't know.'

Rimmer walked in, looking decidedly uncaring. 'Whore cares. Good riddance.'

Lister turned in her chair to look back at him. 'Rimmer, doesn't it make you feel good knowing that somewhere, there's a version of you doing really well?'

'Not really, no. Somewhere, there's a version of me with flippers for hands and three heads. It doesn't mean I want to dwell on it.'

Tyten chimed in. 'But he saved our lives.'

'Oh, he was sooo heroic... his hair swished about as he ran through a meadow! Quite frankly, he was pathetic.'

Lister looked back out of the window ahead of her. 'But he was an adventurer, charting the unknown... never knowing where he was going to end up. It's inspiring.'

'Ugh, vomit city.'

Hab appeared on screen. 'Alright dudes. So now we've got our universe back, should I plot a course back to earth You know... just incase it does still exist?'

'No Hab,' Lister said. 'Don't plot any course. I think I'm just gonna wing it.'

Rimmer looked panicked. 'Um, Lister... what are you doing?'

'Who wants to go home when you've got three million years of space to explore?' She smiled and glanced over at Cat who seemed thrilled at the idea of exploring. 'Cat, hit the reheat. Let's see what's out there!'

## ABOUT THE AUTHOR

Dick Bush works as a writer and director in the adult film industry. He has directed content for Brazzers, Digital Playground, Dorcel, Television X and The Adult Channel. His films include Sherlock XXX - AVN Best Foreign Feature 2017 and The Doctor - AVN Best Foreign Feature 2016. Follow him on twitter @dickbush.